"I don't want to lose you, Kelsey."

Ben's arms tightened around her waist. "When I saw you running toward that burning building, I thought my heart would stop. Kelsey, I wonder if you know just how much you've come to mean to me."

"I know," she whispered, snuggling into his embrace. Her heart ached with love for him. She drew his face close to hers. "I know so well—I feel it, too."

He moaned softly when she kissed him. Within the circle of his arms, Kelsey felt safe, invulnerable, almost giddy with happiness.

But without warning Kelsey's euphoria vanished when she glanced down and saw the gold foil florist box waiting for her on the doorstep. With hands trembling and heart racing, she picked up the long, slim package and pulled back the lid. She held her breath as she peeled the white tissue back to reveal two long-stemmed red roses. Every illusion of safety shattered around her. Two roses meant two days left before a killer caught up to her.

ABOUT THE AUTHOR

Laura Gordon considers herself lucky to live in the shadows of the magnificent Colorado mountains. With the Rockies for inspiration, and her husband and children providing moral support, Laura is a full-time writer with a penchant for romantic suspense. She is happiest when creating characters who face danger and discover that the magic of their once-in-a-lifetime love is worth the risk.

Books by Laura Gordon

HARLEQUIN INTRIGUE
220—DOUBLE BLACK DIAMOND
255—SCARLET SEASON

Don't miss any of our special offers. Write to us at the following address for information on our newest releases.

Harlequin Reader Service
U.S.: 3010 Walden Ave., P.O. Box 1325, Buffalo, NY 14269
Canadian: P.O. Box 609, Fort Erie, Ont. L2A 5X3

Dominoes
Laura Gordon

Harlequin Books

TORONTO • NEW YORK • LONDON
AMSTERDAM • PARIS • SYDNEY • HAMBURG
STOCKHOLM • ATHENS • TOKYO • MILAN
MADRID • WARSAW • BUDAPEST • AUCKLAND

To Mary Ellen O'Neill—for her inestimable expertise, unfaltering faith and special friendship

ISBN 0-373-22282-3

DOMINOES

Sears Tower

Congress Parkway

St. James
Investigations

Clark Street

Printer's Row   Federal Street

CHICAGO

Auditorium
Theatre

Congress Plaza

Grant Park

Lake Michigan

CAST OF CHARACTERS

Kelsey St. James—As a private eye, she'd always been able to find answers for other people; now she needed her own.

Ben Tanner—A detective and a loner who lived by his own rules.

Shannon Hughes—Her death triggered a deadly game of dominoes.

Douglas Hughes—An ex-husband with a grudge and a secret.

Nelson Masters—He was a Milquetoast incarnate, but had he been more than a friend to Shannon?

Cecil Hughes—His weaknesses were deadly... to others.

Roger McElroy—This hard-boiled P.I. gave his profession a bad name.

Gilbert Montoya—A cop with a lot to learn.

Claire Merriweather—Her dancers were her life....

Prologue

Death hovered around her like an impatient suitor. The seeping crimson stain on the asphalt caused the brown hair at the back of her head to appear black. In a matter of moments the long night would be over. At least for Shannon Hughes.

For her murderer, Shannon's death was merely the latest step in an unalterable sequence of events over which he had no control. He still had much to do. Working around Deirdre had never been easy. With a sigh, he bent over the body to complete the ritual.

A sudden noise at the end of the alley echoed through the darkness and prickled up his spine, fine-tuning his already alert senses. His eyes darted toward the sound. In the pool of light from a streetlamp, a group of kids had gathered.

"Hey, man! Whatcha doin' down there?" a young, aggressive male voice demanded.

"Call an ambulance!" Shannon's murderer shouted over his shoulder as he hunched over the lifeless form and pretended to render first aid. His barked command scattered the group like buckshot.

It wasn't panic but irritation he felt when he realized a couple of the kids were running toward him. Before they could reach his side, he ripped the grayish white adhesive from Shannon's mouth with a deft flick of his wrist and stuffed the sticky square into his pocket.

He kept his face averted when a tall kid smelling of cigarettes and beer and dressed in a tattered denim jacket bent down beside him.

The kid's female companion gasped, "Oh, my God!"

"What happened?" the boy asked.

"She jumped," Shannon's killer lied solemnly with an economy of sound. He felt their eyes follow his gaze up the side of the apartment building behind him where individual balconies formed a neat ten-story column.

"Did you see her do it?"

The killer nodded. Indeed he had seen it all.

"Man!" the boy gasped, rising to his feet and backing a few cautious steps away.

"Is she . . . dead?" the girl asked, her voice tremulous.

Bending over the body, careful to keep his face turned away from their startled eyes, the murderer placed a practiced ear on Shannon's motionless chest. Barely able to suppress his sigh of relief, he uttered a somber "Yes."

"Oh, my God!" the girl whispered again. "Let's get out of here, Tommy." She clutched her companion's sleeve. "Come on, please. Let's go!" she urged him when he hesitated. "My mom thinks I'm at a movie. She'll freak if she finds out I'm mixed up in any of this."

"Sorry, man," the boy apologized over his shoulder as the girl tugged him farther down the alley. "Her mom's the nervous type, you know?" The sound of their retreating footsteps echoed across the deserted asphalt as they raced back out into the street.

The killer smiled. It was nice to know that children still cared about their mothers, he thought as he slid into the shadows at the other end of the alley and disappeared into the night. The sound of the sirens in the distance reassured him. His job was finished. At least for tonight.

Chapter One

By midmorning the air was already heavy and damp, a grim preview of what the afternoon held in store for the city's already heat-beleaguered residents.

"Ah, Chicago in July," Kelsey St. James muttered, brushing idly at a honey-colored curl that drooped across her forehead. Her car's air conditioner had conked out somewhere on upper State Street as Kelsey had crept her way through the traffic headed downtown.

The heat clung to her like a sodden sheet as she angled her aging Chevy into a parking space opposite the building that housed her office. Just before shutting off the engine, Kelsey flipped the switch on the fan, only to be rewarded with another blast of warm air—if only the heater had worked so well last winter.

She reached for the overstuffed tote bag and battered briefcase that sat beside her on the seat, and scooping her cargo up into one arm, she clambered out of her car and hurried across the street.

As she had on countless mornings, especially when traffic was snarled, Kelsey remembered how three years ago during her father's first and last visit to her office, he'd declared her location and her choice of buildings unsuitable. He was partially right. The refurbished Printer's Row section of downtown wasn't at all convenient to the suburban neighborhood where she lived. The forty-five-minute drive each way *was* a hassle.

But her father's prediction that her LaSalle Street location would discourage legitimate clients had proved to be groundless. Business was good. The agency was growing. In the past year Kelsey had taken in a lot more work than she'd anticipated.

Shouldering the glass door open and stepping inside the pale brick building, she wondered how her father would have viewed her success if he had lived long enough to see it.

"If he could see me now," she murmured to herself as she glanced down the long, narrow hallway, trying without success to view her surroundings objectively. As it had from the day she'd signed the lease, the building's interior desperately needed a fresh coat of paint. The trail meandering down the center of the avocado green carpet grew more threadbare each day, and overhead, the lights—relics of the fifties—flickered incessantly.

Kelsey glanced at the water-stained acoustic ceiling tile and thought for a moment about relocating her agency. But even as the idea took shape in her mind, the memory of the ordeal she'd endured in finding this place cemented her decision to stay. All that Realtor-induced chaos—who needed it? The day-long marathons from one uptown high rise or suburban office complex to another. The city-wide treks. The guided tours of suites with a view of the city, the lake and the park.

All those views. Ugh! Kelsey's stomach rolled just thinking about those panoramic, high-rise views, the ones that had sent her rushing back downtown as though her life had depended on it. For as unaccustomed as she was to letting anyone or anything set limits on her life, Kelsey St. James had always bowed with grudging acceptance to an unrelenting fear of heights. And because of her old nemesis, the LaSalle Street Building with its unpretentious, one-story humility had been the perfect choice.

Kelsey stopped in front of the first suite on her right, tugged the door open and smiled at the small, dark-haired woman behind the receptionist desk. "Morning, Izzy," she called from the door. "I've got Danish from Volkman's. Come down when you get a minute."

Izzy's smile was warm, but she shook her head wearily. "The doctor's booked all morning, but I'll try to slip down after lunch."

"I'll save a sticky bun for your dessert," Kelsey promised before she slipped back into the hallway.

At the door marked Barber, Kelsey tapped lightly on the glass and held up the Volkman's bag. Sam Bostwick was on the phone and he had a customer waiting in the chair, but he smiled and mouthed the words, "See you later."

A wave of relatively cool air swirled down from the large vent above Sam's door. "Home sweet home," Kelsey murmured as she moved up in front of the last door on the left where the words St. James Investigations were stenciled in black across the frosted pane.

The phone on the other side of the door started ringing as her fingers closed around the doorknob.

When the knob wouldn't turn, she peered through the glass at the empty receptionist's desk and her heart sank. Shannon was late. Again.

As the phone continued to ring, Kelsey's anxious fingers delved to the bottom of her purse for her keys and her irritation increased. What was it going to take for Shannon to take her job seriously? It was almost as though the conversation they'd had last night had never taken place—the conversation Kelsey *wished* had never taken place.

But what choice had Shannon given her? Every other day it seemed there was something else to keep Shannon from the duties she'd been hired to perform.

When Shannon had arrived in Chicago a month ago, the timing had seemed perfect to Kelsey. The caseload at the agency had grown beyond the point that she could handle both the paperwork and the investigations herself. She needed a secretary and Shannon needed a job. What could go wrong? The fact that her old high school chum could neither type nor file seemed merely an incidental inconvenience to Kelsey at the time.

Shaking her head, Kelsey blew out a long exasperated sigh, irritated again by her naivety. She should have known better. She should have known that eventually she'd be forced into acting the part of employer. Surely by this morning, Kelsey tried to tell herself, Shannon would have come to understand her position. But if she had, where was she?

Last night over pizza and wine at Prizzi's, Shannon had seemed to respond to Kelsey's gentle reprimand reasonably well. But even as Shannon had jokingly accused her of "pulling rank," Kelsey could sense her old friend's resentment. There was little about Shannon that escaped Kelsey's naturally intuitive eye. They'd known each other so well for so long—too long to risk their friendship now, Kelsey told herself, agency or no agency.

Finally her fingers closed around the illusive keys, and she jammed them into the lock and shoved the door open, bursting into the room and dropping her bag and her briefcase onto the floor behind the desk as she lunged for the ringing telephone. Held hostage to the receiver, she could only watch as the tote bag toppled, spilling its contents onto the floor beneath the desk.

"St. James Investigations," Kelsey announced breathlessly into the phone. It was going to be the Friday from hell, she warned herself when the second line lit up.

"Kelsey, is that you?" Nelson Masters asked in an anxious tone.

The second line started ringing. "Yes, Nelson. Hold on a sec, okay?" Without waiting for his reply, Kelsey jabbed the hold button and activated the second line. "St. James Investigations. Could you hold, please?" But Kelsey hadn't been fast enough, and the line went dead.

She clicked back to the first line. "Good morning, Nelson," she lied.

"Well, at last. I've been calling since nine. We have an appointment this morning to talk about the VanWaters matter. I hope you haven't forgotten."

"No. I haven't forgotten," she assured him. "But I'm afraid I'm going to have to call you back," she apologized. "Shannon hasn't come in yet and I just walked in the door myself."

"But I was counting on being able to discuss the matter with you now, Kelsey."

She closed her eyes and rolled her fingertips over her lids. Nelson's persistence was leading to a king-size headache. If the high-strung claims investigator for Consolidated Universal Insurance hadn't been singularly responsible for calling the agency in on so many lucrative cases over the past year, Kelsey would have been tempted to cut him off and apologize later.

"After taking another look at our records, I'm more convinced than ever that we have a clear case of fraud here," he continued.

"Nelson," Kelsey broke in. "I don't have the VanWaters paperwork in front of me. Give me a chance to get into my office and I'll pull the file and call you back."

He didn't try to hide his impatience. "Oh, all right," he sighed. "I'll be waiting for your call. And by the way—"

"Hold on, Nelson. I've got another call." Deftly she put Nelson on hold for the second time and activated the other line.

"St. James Investigations."

"Miss St. James?"

Kelsey recognized the voice immediately. "Yes, yes, Dr. Ingersol, it's Kelsey. How is Mr. Chan doing? Is he going to be all right?"

"He's going to be just fine. The scrapes and bruises were superficial. But you know, Kelsey, this operation is something he should've had done long before now."

Kelsey agreed with the doctor, running her fingers nervously through the thick strands of blond hair that brushed her shoulders. "I'll swing by as soon as I can slip away from my office. But if there's any problem, any complication..."

"Someone from my office will call you," the doctor assured her. "Don't worry, I've performed this procedure hundreds of times. It's quite routine."

Despite Dr. Ingersol's reassurances, Kelsey felt an uneasiness churning in her stomach as she disconnected the line and returned to Nelson Masters.

"I really have to go, Nelson," she explained. "I'll look over the VanWaters file and get back to you. I expect Shannon to come charging in any minute and take over the phones." *From my mouth to God's ear,* Kelsey hoped as she hung up the phone. Almost immediately the first line lit up and rang again.

"St. James Investigations. May I help you?" Trying to force a smile into her voice caused Kelsey's words to sound clipped and dry.

"Tell your secretary she's late." The male voice seemed vaguely familiar.

"Who is this?" Kelsey asked, but before she could gather the thoughts the caller's curt message had scattered, the line went dead and the second line rang.

"St. James Invest—no, no this is not the State Unemployment Center." But if this day got any crazier, Kelsey decided as she hung up the phone, she might just look up the number and call them herself. There had to be an easier way to pay the bills.

When the phone lapsed into momentary silence, Kelsey hitched up her denim skirt and dropped down on her hands and knees to retrieve the bag of Danish and the can of diet soda that had rolled under the desk.

When the phone started ringing again, Kelsey uttered one of her grandfather's most colorful curses. Before she could reach for the phone, she felt a sudden rush of air from the hallway.

"Thank God you're here!" she exclaimed without looking up. "Grab the phone, will you? Charlie got into another fight last night and now he's going into surgery, Nelson's having a nervous breakdown, and if I don't get ten minutes away from this phone, I swear I'm going to hurt somebody."

"Sounds desperate." Large, warm, unmistakably male fingers closed around hers as they reached for the pop can at the same time.

Kelsey jerked her hand away and stood up quickly. The phone continued to ring and she reached for it as she took in the bold appearance of the tall, broad-shouldered man standing on the other side of the desk, dressed in jeans and a pale yellow polo shirt and holding her diet soda in one bearlike paw.

The eyes that stared back at her were an unusual and compelling shade of silver gray. His thick lashes and brows were as jet black as the mane of unruly waves that covered his head.

"St. James Investigations," Kelsey said into the phone as she slipped into the chair, unconsciously giving her skirt a tug. "Be with you in a moment," she mouthed to the stranger, breaking eye contact for the first time.

The caller was Shannon's attorney, and Kelsey scribbled the message rapidly before she hung up. A tiny nerve quivered at the corner of her mouth when she turned a professional smile on the man still waiting on the other side of the desk.

An uncomfortable awareness of the effect the stranger seemed to be having on her nervous system rippled through her. "Can I help you with something?" she asked, reaching to retrieve the soda he held out to her. When his fingers grazed hers, his touch sent a sensation zinging through her that went way beyond anything Kelsey could begin to rationalize—especially this morning.

"I hope your friend's surgery is nothing serious," he said.

Kelsey blinked, momentarily confused by his comment until she realized he was referring to what she'd said when she'd thought it had been Shannon coming through the door.

"Oh, you must mean Mr. Chan." She dismissed his concern with a wave of her hand. "He'll be all right. If this operation keeps him home nights, it will be well worth the trouble." She addressed his puzzled expression with a wry smile. "Mr. Chan is a Siamese cat with a case of raging hormones."

His smile was quick and easy, and just warm enough to trip a series of alarms within Kelsey's defense system. Strange, the agency's reception area had always seemed adequate in size before this morning. Now it seemed the walls were closing in.

"Is he in?" the stranger asked, indicating with a lift of one dark brow the closed door to the left of the receptionist's desk.

She frowned. It was a common mistake, the assumption that St. James Investigations was run by a man. But as often as it happened, Kelsey never seemed to get used to it.

"Do you have an appointment?" she asked tersely.

With a fluid movement, the stranger reached into one hip pocket of his snug-fitting jeans and produced a leather badge case, which he opened with a flick of his wrist. "Just tell your boss Detective Tanner would like a moment of his time."

"A cop," Kelsey muttered, shaking her head. "I should have known." She thought she detected a flicker of reaction in his eyes, although his self-assured expression hadn't changed perceptibly. "Detective Tanner," she said, rising, "I'm Kelsey St. James." For some reason she resisted offering him her hand. "The sole owner of this agency. The boss," she added with a cool smile. "Now, tell me what can St. James Investigations do to assist Chicago's finest this morning?"

If she'd disturbed his mental equilibrium for even the space of a heartbeat, it didn't show. "St. James," he said thoughtfully. "Any relation to Chief—"

"His daughter," she offered curtly. This, too, happened far more often than Kelsey would have liked, and she braced for what came next—the look of open admiration and respect, followed by the same old tired questions about what it had been like growing up with a father like Police Chief Jake St. James, a Chicago legend.

But Detective Tanner surprised her again by merely noting, "He was a good cop," as he replaced his badge in his back pocket.

His expression grew deadly serious, and he shifted his stance slightly, which made him seem somehow more official and commanded Kelsey's full attention.

"I'm afraid I have some bad news concerning one of your employees, Shannon Hughes."

Kelsey's stomach pitched and she felt the blood draining from her face. "Shannon?" Unconsciously she reached for the desk top to steady herself. "What happened?" she asked. "Has there been an accident? Is she all right?"

His expression changed only slightly, but Kelsey intercepted its dark meaning immediately. Her eyelids fluttered and the breath whooshed out of her in a gasp.

In the next moment he was beside her. "Sit down," he ordered gently, pulling the chair away from the desk and easing her into it.

"Please," she demanded in a ragged whisper, "please tell me what's happened."

He hesitated for only the breadth of a second before he said, "An ambulance was called to the alley behind her apartment building late last night." His words were startlingly official, yet something in his tone remained gentle and sympathetic. "They tried to revive her...but it was too late."

The world spun out of control. Kelsey's confused thoughts floundered somewhere between stunned disbelief and overwhelming pain. "No!" she shouted, jumping to her feet and shoving past him toward the door. "There must be some mistake."

Before he could respond, she shouted again, "It's a mistake! I was with Shannon last night. We had dinner, we talked...she was fine. Just fine! You must have the wrong person. This is all just some horrible mixup!" Her eyes pleaded with him to say or do something to break the grip of the invisible fist that crushed her heart.

"There's been no mistake, Ms. St. James," he said in a low voice. For a moment they stood staring at each other, two strangers numbed by the tension of the emotional strain that twisted between them.

"I'm sorry," he said quietly. "Sit down, Ms. St. James," he ordered gently as he put his arm around her shoulders and led her back to the desk.

Despite the fact that he was a total stranger and a cop, Kelsey allowed herself to be led like a frightened child. For a moment she longed to let him take over, to shrink behind the boundary of his cool objectivity and professional strength. His steady presence seemed the only barrier between herself and a waking nightmare too horrible to comprehend. Her knees folded involuntarily as she sank down into the chair.

Shannon is dead, a dreadful inner voice whispered. Her body shuddered with each word as images flickered through her mind like an old newsreel, presenting a montage of the past: Shannon dressed in a varsity sweater and pleated skirt at the senior homecoming game, Shannon on her wedding day, a blur of smiles and white satin. And finally, most cruelly vivid, were the images of Shannon as she had looked last night, with her expression of anger and resentment.

It had been their first real argument, Kelsey realized. And now this stranger, this cop, was telling her it would be their last.

Kelsey leaned over the desk and buried her face in her hands. Would the images of a lifetime friendship be forever tainted by their last awful night together? "Dear God," she whispered, "this can't be happening."

She felt his hand on her shoulder. "I'm sorry," he said again.

The tears slid silently from her eyes as she reached for the handkerchief he offered. Later she would remember its comforting sun-dried scent as she brought it to her eyes.

When the phone rang, he picked it up, and fresh pain stabbed her when she heard him say Shannon wasn't in. Kelsey drew a shaky breath and closed her eyes again, trying desperately to maintain her composure. When she opened her eyes, she found him studying the framed picture that sat beside the phone, the picture of Shannon and her, both smiling, arms linked.

"Perhaps I should come back later," he said.

Kelsey shook her head. "No. Stay. Other than her father, I'm the closest thing Shannon has—" her voice cracked and she swallowed hard "—that she had to family. Please tell me what happened." No matter how painful it was, Kelsey had to know.

For the first time, his steady scrutiny wavered and fell away from her face.

"Tell me," she demanded again. "I have a right to know."

When his eyes rose to meet hers again, something haunted in his expression caused her to hold her breath. Her fingers dug into the vinyl arms of the chair as she braced for the worst.

Chapter Two

"Suicide?" The word emerged a strangled whisper. "No, no, she couldn't have," she cried, closing her eyes, trying to dispel the nightmare Ben Tanner presented as reality. Though Kelsey fought it, denied it with every ounce of loyalty she possessed, the possibility that Shannon had taken her own life slipped into her consciousness with the insidious skill of a deadly reptile. Her head throbbed and the searing lump in her throat refused to be dislodged.

"As difficult as it may be for you to accept, it's a possibility we have to consider," Ben explained quietly.

Kelsey's eyes snapped open. "Well, I won't consider it!" she shot back bitterly. "Not for a minute."

"You'd known Shannon Hughes for a long time."

"Forever," she said. "In fact, I can't remember ever *not* knowing Shannon. We grew up in the same small town, went to the same school." They'd shared each girlish heartthrob and heartache, every crazy hope and scheme for the future. And in the end, they'd shared a friendship that had endured time and distance when they'd chosen separate paths after high school graduation—Shannon into marriage and a move to the affluent suburbs, Kelsey to pursue a criminal-justice degree in the heart of Chicago.

"Had you noticed any differences in the last few days or weeks in her behavior?" Ben asked, tugging Kelsey back to the present.

She shook her head, but the angry words that had flown between Shannon and her echoed cruelly through her mind. "She was going through some rough times, but she wasn't despondent, if that's what you're getting at."

He didn't push her for more. He seemed to have all the time in the world, and for that, at least, Kelsey was grateful. Ben Tanner was a cop, a complete stranger, but a part of her dreaded the time when he would leave and she'd be left alone to face the remainder of this wretched day alone.

"What else can you tell me about Shannon that might help us piece together what happened to her?"

When Kelsey wondered how best to describe her friend, the words intelligent, loyal and irreverent came to mind first. "She was a very special person," she said. "Tough. Resilient. The eternal optimist. Her mother died in an accident when Shannon was only twelve. Her father has spent the past fifteen years trying to forget." Shannon and Kelsey had both experienced the loss of a father—Shannon's to a bottle, Kelsey's to a badge.

"Was she having financial problems?" he asked.

"She was recovering from the legal expenses of her divorce," Kelsey offered reluctantly. "It wasn't easy for her," she added, resenting the mental note he made.

"But Shannon knew how to take care of herself. She wasn't desperate."

Though it had been difficult for her, Shannon had been forced to come to Kelsey, asking for financial help more than once in the past. If she'd been desperate, she'd have asked again, wouldn't she?

"This past year had been especially tough for her," she said quietly, wondering for whose benefit she was explaining. She went on to tell him about Shannon's recent move to Chicago, and her words seemed to flow of their own accord, tumbling over each other. She couldn't seem to stop them, and for some strange reason she didn't want to try.

"The divorce was bitter," she said. Shannon had come out the loser in the "house-wars," as she'd jokingly called them whenever she referred to the property battle in which she and Douglas had been engaged for the past twelve months.

"But she was coping—" Kelsey stopped cold. *Coping*. Had that word ever sounded more cold and impersonal? "She was trying to pull her life back together," she amended.

How well she remembered the day Shannon had moved into the one-bedroom apartment in Lakeview. "She loved her new place." Kelsey's voice faded, her thoughts shuddering away from the French doors in the living room that opened onto a balcony suspended ten stories above the ground.

"You mentioned a gap of several years when you weren't in close contact with Shannon."

"A gap in terms of miles, maybe," she allowed. "But Shannon and I always kept in touch." Not nearly as close as Kelsey would have liked, she admitted to herself now. Part of the problem had been Douglas, a possessive and domineering spouse who believed that he and he alone belonged at the center of Shannon's universe. He'd done little through the years to hide his disapproval of his wife's best friend. It seemed to Kelsey that Douglas was afraid that some of Kelsey's independence might rub off on his wife. And in the end, it had been that controlling and possessive behavior that had cost him his marriage.

"Did anything unusual happen last night?" Ben asked, tugging Kelsey out of her dark reverie and into the bright pain of the present. "An argument with her ex? A disagreement with a new boyfriend?"

Kelsey shook her head, but even as she did, her thoughts flashed back to something Shannon had mentioned jokingly about receiving flowers from a "secret admirer," something about roses and a card with a riddle. Kelsey wished she could remember more of what Shannon had said, but Ben's next question shattered her thoughts. "Was she having problems here at work?" he asked.

Kelsey's throat went dry and her heart thudded against her chest; his probing had come too painfully close to the truth. "Shannon and I had words last night," she admitted, an overwhelming inner ache robbing her voice of its natural brightness. "She'd been coming in late," she explained. "It was happening more and more often. Sometimes she didn't show up at all. It reached the point where I felt I had to say something." Her justifications sounded as empty as the dark void she felt growing in the pit of her stomach.

"I see," he said evenly.

"No, you don't." Kelsey rose quickly and walked over to the window to stare out onto the street with blurred eyes. "It isn't what you're thinking."

"And just what am I thinking?"

She swiped at her tears and spun around to face him, expecting to find a smug stare, but instead his expression was one of sympathetic concern. Kelsey's world tilted again. How did one handle a man whose reactions were so unpredictable?

"Shannon was human," she said. "She got mad. Sometimes she got depressed. Who doesn't? But she didn't stay down for long. Even when times were the roughest with Douglas..."

"Her ex?"

Kelsey nodded and frowned at the picture of the tall, blond, self-assured Douglas Hughes that formed in her mind. "She was always so positive, so sure things would work out."

"You know, some people manage to keep their feelings hidden even from their closest friends."

She shook her head, and despite the grim circumstances, she smiled wistfully, remembering her friend's animated personality. "When Shannon Hughes was upset, the whole world knew, but when she was happy, everyone was invited to share in the party." Her voice cracked.

"Take it easy," Ben said, moving up beside her. "I know how tough this is for you."

Kelsey swallowed a bitter rejoinder. He was only trying to help, of course, but how could he begin to know how she felt, how deep her loss went, how bitter the guilt that haunted her?

"My friend did not kill herself, Detective Tanner," she declared evenly, brushing past him as she moved back to the desk.

He studied her for a long moment without saying a word.

"I'd like to see a copy of the police report."

His silvery eyes narrowed. "The report isn't finished. There are still many unanswered questions."

Kelsey opened her mouth to speak, but he didn't give her the chance. "She didn't leave a note," he explained. His expression was grim. "They usually leave a note."

They! Kelsey thought, resentment slithering through her. Obviously to the overworked, understaffed Chicago Police Department, and to Detective Ben Tanner, as well, Shannon had already become merely another faceless statistic.

"Is there anyone you'd like me to call?" he asked.

Kelsey shook her head. No doubt the police had already contacted Shannon's father, but she would have to call Douglas. Then there was Shannon's attorney, Vanessa Overholt, and eventually Nelson Masters and the other business associates with whom Shannon had worked directly.

A sinking feeling of renewed sadness engulfed her when Kelsey realized that Shannon really hadn't been in town long enough to make many new friends.

"Then I guess that's all for now, Ms. St. James," he said. "If you remember anything later or you'd just like to talk, don't hesitate to give me a call."

He handed her a card, and she stared at it a moment with unseeing eyes. Suddenly, like a sleepwalker jolted awake, Kelsey's head snapped up and she declared, "I *will* be calling you, Detective Tanner. You can bank on it." She barely recognized the angry voice as her own. "And when I call I'll have a list of questions stretching from here to City Hall. And I'll expect straight answers."

The spark she saw glinting in his unwavering stare told her Ben Tanner was unaccustomed to being challenged. Kelsey felt her own resolve tighten in her chest. Maybe it was shock or misplaced anger or her own nagging guilt. Or maybe it was having survived childhood as a hardheaded cop's only daughter. But whatever it was that caused her reaction, Kelsey welcomed it, welcomed the temporary strength it afforded her as she matched his steady stare without flinching.

"Shannon Hughes did not commit suicide, Tanner, and I won't accept anyone saying she did." With sudden clarity, Kelsey realized that until she knew how and why Shannon had died, her own life would hold little meaning. "I want to know how...it happened," she said, her voice ragged. "Every detail. I want a copy of your report."

"I'm afraid that isn't possible," he said.

"Don't try to stonewall me, Detective," she warned. "I want to see that report and I will, with or without your help."

When the phone rang, the sound punctured the air like a small explosion. Kelsey imagined for a moment that the tension sparking between them might burst into sudden flames. The phone rang a second time, and still neither of them moved. With the third ring, Kelsey blinked. She found she couldn't say a word when Tanner picked up the phone, listened a moment and then announced flatly that St. James Investigations was closed for the day. Then, with an efficient movement, he replaced the receiver noiselessly and flipped the switch to turn the ringer off.

How was it possible, Kelsey wondered, to feel as though she wanted to punch the guy at one moment and in the next feel as though she owed him a debt of gratitude?

"Your friend's death is still under police investigation, Ms. St. James," he said evenly, his smoky gaze holding hers. "We don't have all the answers yet, but right now it looks as though we're dealing with accidental death or suicide."

"Was there a witness?"

For a moment he seemed to be deciding whether or not to answer her. "A couple of teenagers called the ambulance."

"Have you talked to them? What did they say? What did they see?"

"They said she jumped," he said quietly, his eyes still locked on her face.

Kelsey inhaled a sharp, stinging breath. "Give me their names," she demanded, fighting the quaver in her voice as she reached for a pen.

"You know I can't do that."

"Can't? Or won't?" she challenged.

The intensity of his gaze held her temporarily paralyzed. "You know I can't give out that kind of information."

He was right. She knew full well he couldn't give her the names of the witnesses, especially since they were underage, but her frustration flared white-hot. "Damn it, Tanner, I have a right to some answers!"

"And you know I can't give you the ones you want." His words came from immobile lips. His self-assured presence seemed to fill the room again, stealing the oxygen Kelsey so desperately needed to clear her muddled senses.

"In my business," she said, her voice sounding not half as steady as she would have liked, "I've discovered that there are any number of ways to gather information about a case. I'll work around you if I have to."

"I'll just bet you will," he muttered, a frown curling his generous lips and a cynical glint flickering in his dark eyes. "I'm sorry for your loss," he said as he turned and walked toward the door, "but I wouldn't advise that you attempt to interfere with police procedures." Just before striding out the doorway he added, "You know you wouldn't be the first PI to risk losing a license by trying to circumvent the law, Ms. St. James." And, with that blatant warning, he was gone.

"Cops!" she shouted. How they loved to have the last word. "And you, Detective Tanner, wouldn't be the first cop in Chicago to make a damn big mistake!" Her words bounced off the door and echoed around the empty room.

Kelsey slammed her hand down onto the desk. His arrogance was infuriating. Her hand stung, but she didn't care—the pain seemed to give her anger a focus. Her only regret was that Ben Tanner had left before he'd heard her final words.

Kelsey snatched up the phone and defiantly shoved the switch back on. Oh, why the hell did she even care what he'd heard or hadn't heard, she asked herself miserably as she sank down into the chair and buried her head in her hands.

What difference did it make what he or anyone else thought? Shannon was gone. As unbelievable and unfair as it was, it was still true and the reality settled in the pit of Kelsey's stomach.

When the door swung open again, she jerked her head up in startled surprise. Ben Tanner's broad-shouldered frame filled the doorway. His eyes had changed from liquid smoke to steel, and his square jaw seemed set in granite. At that moment Kelsey knew he'd heard every word of her parting shot.

Involuntarily, she winced as he stepped into the room.

"You're right," he said quietly, his gaze fastened on hers. "I guess I wouldn't be the first Chicago cop to make a mistake. As a matter of fact, some would say I've already made more than my share." As he stared at her, an uncertain silence quivered between them and Kelsey held her breath.

With grace unexpected for a man his size, Ben closed the door behind him and moved toward her. For one irrational moment, she felt an almost irrepressible urge to run. But she held her ground, fingers digging new trenches into the padded arms of the chair.

When he spoke again, she felt her heart thudding with each word that came rumbling from deep within his ample chest. "I guess if she'd been my best friend, I could do no less than what you're prepared to do."

In a day filled with shocks that had bombarded her senses like no other day Kelsey could ever remember experiencing, this unexpected reaction from Detective Ben Tanner came as yet another jolt.

"I can't let you see that report," he reminded her, "but I promise to keep you updated on the details. I'll work with you if you'll work with me, providing me with information about your friend."

Kelsey thought she must have heard him wrong. She stared at him unblinking as cautious relief rippled through her, draining the last of her physical and emotional strength. Her muscles ached as though she'd been engaged in some grueling physical battle.

"I won't let you get in my way, and I won't be pushed," he warned, "but if your friend didn't kill herself and her fall wasn't an accident, then someone murdered her. And I promise you I'll do everything I can to find out who that someone was. It's my job and I'm pretty good at it."

She found his intense gaze and the deep timbre of his voice nearly hypnotic. A choked "Thank you" was all she could manage.

In the next moment the door closed behind him and the room seemed to sag with his leaving. Kelsey exhaled a long, ragged breath, leaned her head against the back of the chair and closed her eyes against the grim realities of the morning that continued to wash over her in small tortuous waves.

When the phone rang, Kelsey's reaction was immediate, and her arm shot out to send the offending instrument clattering to the floor. It was a full minute before she started to cry and a good long hour before she stopped.

OUTSIDE THE BUILDING that housed St. James Investigations, Ben flipped his car's air conditioner on high and adjusted the vents on the dash so that the cold air hit his face fully before pulling out into traffic.

"Good job, Tanner," he muttered. Just what the hell had he gotten himself into, he wondered as he drove, his promise to work with Kelsey St. James still ringing in his ears.

He wasn't easily taken in. He didn't bite when baited. And most of all, he didn't bend his own rules, the rules he'd decided long ago worked best for him, the rules that kept him sharp and objective and detached.

But a few minutes ago, making promises to Kelsey St. James, he'd felt anything but objective, anything but detached.

And the feeling was still with him half an hour later, nagging him as he walked down the hallway of the precinct station toward his office.

"Find your PI?" The disembodied voice of Gil Montoya emerged from behind the sports page.

"Yeah," Ben muttered, stopping in front of Gil's desk to pick up the stack of papers and files lying in a basket on one crowded corner of the desk.

"The coroner's report on Hughes came in about an hour ago. It's in there."

"Thanks. Have you read it yet?"

"Yeah." The newspaper collapsed and a startlingly boyish face, framed by a thick crop of straight, dark hair, appeared. "I wrote up a summary of the pathologist's findings. It's attached."

"My PI claims her friend was murdered," Ben said without looking up.

"Smart gal."

Ben's narrowed eyes posed his questions.

"The coroner says our so-called witnesses were wrong."

Ben stalked into his office, flipping through the stack of files, searching for the one marked Hughes. Gil followed, folding his six-one frame into the metal chair by the door.

"They found bruises that had nothing to do with the fall. None of them were really severe, but they were in all the right places."

Ben scanned the report. Gil's condensed version matched exactly.

"There were traces of adhesive around her mouth. She was close to suffocation at the time of the fall. Somebody helped her over that railing, Ben." Gil's voice was solemn.

"Tissue under her nails," Ben noted in a low voice as he read on. "She put up a fight."

Gil stood up. "Yeah," he said at the door as he turned to leave. "But she lost."

Ben released a long, tired sigh as he closed the door behind Gil. He glanced down at the open file again. He would spend a good part of the day reading and re-reading the coroner's report. Though at first glance it looked as though Gil hadn't missed anything, he'd been working as Ben's assistant for just a little over six months. And although Gil was in his early thirties, he was still a rookie, at least to homicide.

Ben stared at the report without picking it up. Though he knew it would bring her little solace, he told himself he should call Kelsey St. James and tell her she'd been right. Shannon Hughes had been murdered.

Kelsey's wealth of inside information concerning Shannon's life-style, her friends and her enemies could prove an invaluable resource for his investigation, Ben reminded himself. He should call her and make arrangements to meet, the sooner the better, before the killer's trail grew stale.

But instead of reaching for the phone, Ben flipped the file closed and sank back down into his chair. At the moment, something inside him resisted doing what he knew he should.

With his chin resting on steepled fingers, he swiveled around in his chair and turned his back to his desk to gaze out the window behind him. The unrelenting summer sun sent its rays glinting off granite and steel, sending lasers of light to pierce the heat that rose in liquid waves off the pavement. On the street, pedestrians clung to the meager shadows of an occasional storefront awning, venturing out only long enough to welcome the artificial breeze of passing cars and buses.

Ben stared at the heat-blanched city scene without seeing. His gaze was fixed on the past as he relived what had occurred the last time he'd been foolish enough to join forces with a private investigator.

An investigative specialist, Roger McElroy had billed himself—Peeping Tom would have been a more apt description. Ben should have known better. Every instinct had warned him that the PI was trouble, despite the fact that McElroy was licensed and well-known to other cops who had used his services in the past, bartered with him for information and vouched for his reliability.

When McElroy had contacted Ben, he'd claimed to be in contact with a source who had information about a murder that had taken place during a drug deal gone sour. It was a case that Ben took personally. Was there any other way to take it when a child was involved?

In this particular case it had been a nine-year-old girl who'd taken the stray bullet. Ben swore softly under his breath. Five years had passed, and still the anger surged through him whenever he thought about the girl's family.

Ben had wanted the contact that McElroy promised. He had wanted the lead badly enough to ignore his instincts. Eventually he'd given the PI inside information about the case in exchange for a meeting with the informant.

He winced, remembering. At the arranged meeting, the informant had panicked, pulled a gun and fired. Ben had been hit. McElroy had run, leaving Ben alone and bleeding in a Southside alleyway.

Three weeks later, laid up in a hospital bed, recovering from a gunshot that should have killed him, Ben vowed never to break his own rules again. He'd listened to his instincts and trusted his gut ever since.

Even though he'd eventually been a principal player in the apprehension of the girl's murderer, and Roger McElroy had been cleared of all suspicion regarding his involvement with the incident, the lessons Ben had learned in that Southside alleyway were ones he swore he'd never forget: PIs were a different breed; they didn't operate by the same code as cops. A smart cop didn't trust one at his back.

Then why trust Kelsey St. James? he asked himself as he spun around in his chair to stare down at the Hughes file again. He couldn't deny something inside him had responded to the golden-haired lady with the incredibly blue eyes. Something deep inside him had been moved in a way he hadn't been moved in a long time. Maybe ever. And maybe it was that last thought that disturbed him the most.

For it wasn't merely his promise to let her in on his investigation that troubled him, and he knew it. It was Kelsey St. James herself who had so dramatically affected his equilibrium. But what made him think she'd operate any differently than others in her field? Because she was a female? Because she was beautiful? Because she had what was more than likely a fatal blind spot where her friends were concerned?

Ben stood up and paced across the room. Surely it would take more than a pair of beautiful baby blues and the best set of legs in Chicago to make him forget a lesson so bitterly learned, wouldn't it?

Exasperated, Ben sat back down, flipped open the file and tried to focus on the coroner's report. This time would be different, he told himself. This time he'd have to be sure. If his association with Kelsey St. James could help him catch a killer, so be it. If in the meantime she proved to be a straight shooter, then so much the better. Time would tell.

For now, Ben told himself he couldn't afford to ignore his own blind spots, the ones he hadn't even known existed until this morning. After all, what choice did he have in light of the phone call he'd intercepted this morning at the office of St. James Investigations? The one that had come from none other than Private Investigator Roger McElroy himself.

TWO HOURS LATER, Kelsey stood watching two policemen gathering evidence in her office. She felt nearly invisible, her nervous system somehow numbed and deadened by the incomprehensible events of the day. First the horrible news of Shannon's death and now this.

There had been no vandalism, no obvious evidence that a crime had even occurred. The small window above her desk was still locked. The lock on the door that led out to the reception area hadn't been violated. But, despite all appearances, a crime *had* occurred. Kelsey's private office had been burgled.

A short hour ago, after having concluded a very difficult conversation with Shannon's father, Kelsey had called her answering service to inform them that the agency would be closed until Wednesday. She'd been on her way out when she'd met Nelson Masters in the hall.

Nelson had explained how he'd been trying to reach her, but to no avail. In frustration, he'd finally decided to drive over and pick up the VanWaters file himself.

He was the first person Kelsey had had to tell about Shannon's death. And judging by his stricken expression, Kelsey began to wonder if Nelson had been harboring feelings for Shannon that went beyond a casual business relationship.

Kelsey glanced over her shoulder at Nelson now, and realized that if not for him she still might not know her office had been burgled—and at this point, with the tension burning between her shoulders and her head aching, she honestly didn't know whether or not to thank him.

The tall, sandy-haired insurance adjuster sat quietly in the corner, seeming oblivious to the commotion around him as he studied the file he'd come to collect. She envied the distraction his dedication afforded him.

"So you and Mr. Masters were the only ones inside your inner office today, right, ma'am?"

Kelsey nodded in response to the officer's question.

"Anybody besides you and your receptionist have a key?" the shorter of the two policemen asked.

"No one." Her voice was hoarse. Thoughts of Shannon caused a stubborn lump to form again in her throat, and she swallowed hard trying to dislodge it.

"What about a janitor or a maintenance man?"

Kelsey's laugh was curt and humorless. "We don't have any of those services in this building, Officer."

"And no security system, either, I suppose?" At the sound of Ben's voice behind her, Kelsey jumped, her jangled nerves startled. But for some reason, when she whirled around to face him, she had the astonishing sensation she'd just been thrown a lifeline.

"Right. And no security system, either." She managed to offer him a weak smile.

When he motioned to her, she joined him in the hallway.

"Why are *you* here, Detective?" she asked. "I thought your area was homicide."

"It is, but the precinct is a lot like a small town," he explained. "Word gets around. When I heard about the break-in, I thought maybe you could use a familiar face. When did it happen?" he asked.

She shrugged. "Last night, as far as we can tell. Shortly after you left this morning, I decided to close the agency until after the... funeral. I was on my way out when Nelson came in." She tilted her head in the direction of the well-dressed young man still absorbed in the VanWaters file. "I went into my office to get a file for Nelson. At first I didn't notice anything unusual, but when I started looking for the papers we needed, I realized that things had been moved around, rearranged. It was Nelson who discovered the empty petty-cash box buried beneath some papers in the trash can."

"How much money was taken?"

"Not very much. I never kept more than ten or fifteen dollars around. Dr. Faharzadeh's office down the hall and the barber shop next door would have been much better targets if robbery was the motive."

"You said your files were rearranged? How?"

"They were jumbled." With a fresh twinge of grief, Kelsey remembered how Shannon had laughed, throwing up her hands in mock despair at Kelsey's suggestion that she begin tackling the mountain of paper piled on top of the filing cabinets in her private office. "They were all mixed up," she continued, "as though someone had been rummaging through them, searching for something in a hurry."

"Couldn't a mix-up like that have happened during the course of your daily business activities?"

"Absolutely. It happens all the time. Most days I wouldn't have even noticed. But this time was different."

Ben had been standing with feet apart and arms crossed, but when he shifted his weight and leaned one hip against the wall, their shoulders touched. He was so close that Kelsey could almost count the streaks of silver in his smoky eyes.

"What was different about the files today, Kelsey?" he asked.

"The difference was Izzy—my friend Isabella, Dr. Faharzadeh's secretary," she explained. "Shannon and Izzy worked all day yesterday getting those files in order. Izzy is a real expert at organization," she added. "She even taught a Saturday class once at City College on how to reorganize your life." It had been Shannon's idea to ask Izzy to help set up a filing system that would work *for* them instead of *against* them.

"Shannon and Izzy sorted and rearranged everything in my office, including the files. When they finished, things had never looked so good. For the first time in three years I could lay my hands on exactly what I was looking for without a massive search."

"Are any of the files missing?"

"I haven't been able to find out yet," Kelsey replied. The weight of her concern made her voice sound unnaturally low. The information in her clients' files was highly personal and confidential. "Your friends weren't eager for me to do any more damage than I'd already done to whatever evidence might still be available. Later, I'll have to conduct a thorough inventory. But at first glance it doesn't look like anything is missing except the money... and maybe—" She hesitated.

"What else?"

"Oh, I don't know," she said, shaking her head uncertainly. "I might have mislaid them. Or maybe Shannon picked them up on her way out last night."

"What?" Ben pressed. "If you even suspect something else is missing, we need to know."

Kelsey eyed him for an uneasy moment before admitting, "I get nervous when I fly."

He lifted one dark brow quizzically. "Airsick?"

"It has more to do with the altitude. Anyway, I had been planning to fly to New York on Monday and yesterday I picked up some medicine at the pharmacy."

"Motion-sickness pills?"

She nodded. "My doctor prescribes them. They're a bit stronger than the over-the-counter kind. I'm almost sure I left the bottle on top of the file cabinet when I left last night."

"Did you tell them?" he asked, indicating the officers still working inside the office.

She nodded. "They didn't seem overly concerned."

Ben asked her for the name of the medication, and he wrote it down in a small notebook. Idly she watched him write, admiring the large, confident sweeps that formed each letter. "I'm having a difficult time picturing a junkie breaking into your office for fifteen dollars and some motion-sickness pills when there's a doctor's office less than twenty feet away."

Ben put his notebook away as Nelson walked out of the office, briefcase in hand. "Did you get the information you needed?" Kelsey asked him.

"Yes. Thanks," he said quietly, his long face looking especially drawn and haggard. "I know this has been a terrible day for you—for all of us. If I hadn't really needed this information before Monday, I wouldn't have bothered you."

"I know," she assured him, placing a hand gently on his sleeve. After introducing the two men, Kelsey added, "Actually, it's probably a good thing you showed up when you did, Nelson. Any evidence we might find now could have been obliterated by next week."

"Well, if there's anything, anything at all I can do, I hope you'll call me, Kelsey."

She nodded. After a moment of uncomfortable silence, Nelson turned to leave. "You'll let me know... when the service is scheduled?" The last of the color had drained from his face, and in his pale blue eyes Kelsey saw a reflection of grief.

"Of course," Kelsey said softly.

Ben and Kelsey stood in silence watching Nelson leave the building before Ben asked, "Did Shannon have the keys to your office with her when she left last night?"

"I assume she did. Why do you ask?"

Kelsey saw he was measuring his response and wondered why until all at once it hit her, and another jagged piece of an already impossible puzzle presented itself in her mind. "You think Shannon's death and the break-in are in some way related, don't you?" she asked.

"Maybe."

"Then you no longer believe Shannon committed suicide."

He stared at her a long moment before he said, "The coroner's report was waiting for me when I got back to my office. One of the reasons I drove back over here was to give you the results."

Kelsey felt as though all the air had been sucked out of her lungs.

"You were right" was all he said, and Kelsey wondered how he knew that even those few words were almost more than she could bear to hear?

"Murdered?" she whispered.

He nodded, his generous mouth tightening into a hard thin line. "I don't believe in coincidences, Kelsey," he said. "I want you to be very careful until we can get some kind of lead on what's happened."

An icy chill enveloped her as the implication of his words tightened an invisible circle of fear around her heart. Her best friend had been murdered. Her agency had been burgled. And Ben Tanner wasn't the only one who didn't believe in coincidences.

Chapter Three

The adhesive that had stifled the woman's screams as she'd fallen to her death on Thursday was still in his pocket on Monday. He toyed with it as he walked, noting with idle curiosity that it had retained its stickiness. It really *did* pay to use only the best quality, he noted with pride.

Mother always told him any job worth doing was worth doing right, and even as a child he'd taken his parent's words to heart.

Deirdre nudged his shoulder. "Penny for your thoughts."

"Just daydreaming," he replied.

She insisted on remaining a maddening half step behind him as they crossed the grassy expanse. As a result, whenever he turned to look at her, the glaring afternoon sunlight reduced her fine features to nothing more than a faceless silhouette steeped in black.

How could he have been so stupid that he'd have forgotten his sunglasses, he scolded himself. Already pinpricks of pain were beginning behind his left eye. The inevitable agony, added to Deirdre's frequent references to his physical limitations, should have served as sufficient reminders. What was he, some kind of vampire? she'd scoffed.

But today he had more to think about than his glasses, concerns far more important than his chronic photosensitivity, or even Deirdre's sarcasm. Much more important concerns, he reminded himself as he stole a glance at the pretty blonde standing with her back to him just across the way beside the open grave. Again he thought about the adhesive in his pocket and the remainder of the unused roll in his bureau drawer.

"Why did you want to meet here, of all places?" he asked Deirdre without turning around to face her.

"Keep your voice down," she chided over his shoulder. "Have you no respect for the dead?"

"But why here?" he demanded, though he heeded her reprimand and dropped his voice in deference to the small group of mourners gathered a few dozen feet away.

"I thought you might want to pay your last respects." Her remark had its desired effect; a shiver prickled up his spine like an icy finger, despite the heat and humidity that clung to him like a clammy cloth.

"Where's Mother, Deirdre?" he asked, his voice a rough whisper. "I'd hoped you would bring her with you." It had been such a long time since he'd seen her.

"Oh, please," she groaned. "Don't start with all of that again. You'll see her in good time. All in good time. And will you please stop calling me by that wretched name?"

He sensed her irritation, but he didn't care. To him, she would always be Deirdre. Her assumed name, the one she'd taken all those years ago, still didn't come naturally to him. Why she'd changed her name in the first place, how she could have so capriciously disregarded Mother's feelings, was beyond his understanding.

"Now listen to me," she ordered. "We can't stay here long. I need to get back to Mother. And I'm sure you have work to do."

He acknowledged her wisdom with grudging silence.

"Have you found her? The next one?"

He forced himself not to stare at the blonde.

"Well, have you found her or not?"

He shrugged and clamped his teeth together to hide his agitation. Her interrogation scalded him. Did she really think he'd tell her his plans? Did she really think he was that stupid?

"Well?" she prodded, tapping her small foot impatiently.

"I don't answer to you, Deirdre." His comments caused his pulse to quicken. He knew that eventually Deirdre would realize he'd located the next woman on his list, but for now, the freedom to keep his own counsel for just a bit longer gave him a heady feeling of control. And he longed to be in control, if only for a few more precious days.

"You haven't found her, have you? Good. Maybe you've given this whole thing up. If that's the case, I'm glad you've come to your senses," she said, but there was an absence of sincerity in her voice, and he couldn't help but wonder if she was mocking him. "Mother will be so pleased."

"When can I talk to her?" The pressure continued to build behind his eye, the startling pinwheels of pain becoming brighter. It was hopeless to try to look at her as long as she persisted in standing in the sun. But then, he really didn't need to see her face, he told himself bitterly, to envision her taunting smile.

"I told you, Mother has a lot of work to do. Now don't nag. Behave yourself. I'll be in touch with you soon," she said, her tone patronizing. "And by the way, Mother does send her best."

Was he supposed to thank her for this morsel, he wondered angrily. "Don't push me, *Deirdre,*" he threatened, his voice a low hiss as he spat out her forsaken name.

"My, my, it sounds as though someone may be coming down with a case of nerves. Perhaps these little nighttime diversions of yours are getting the best of you."

"Oh, for God's sake," he exploded. "Why won't you just leave me alone?" The pain behind his eye spread in pulsating waves through his neck and shoulders.

"Very well. I'm going, but you needn't be so rude," she scolded.

He sensed her moving away, and he felt relieved. But as always his relief was tinged with remorse. Why must it be this way? he asked himself.

With one hand pressed against his temple, he turned and watched her moving steadily away from him until she was merely a graceful shadow rippling over the grass. He made the decision to go after her, reminding himself it only made things worse when they quarreled.

He sighed wearily as he walked. Some things never changed, he told himself. The outcome of their encounters was always the same. Somehow the unspoken rules of their relationship had been set long ago, and through the years nothing had changed: Deirdre was always the one who walked away and he was always the one to follow. And in all these years, he felt certain she'd never even bothered to look back to make sure.

Once he'd found her relentless confidence a source of strength. But lately their encounters had left him feeling increasingly defensive and bitter. She had a way of diminishing him, making him feel incompetent, bumbling and unworthy. Time and again, he felt he had to prove his worth.

Although it wasn't Deirdre's criticisms, but rather Mother's convictions, he realized, that had nurtured his dogged devotion to perfection. "Everyone has their particular gift," she had told him as he'd sat on the sidelines watching Deirdre in the spotlight. "You're special," she'd said. "Your very best is all you have to offer. Remember that always." And he had. Just as he had always remembered her chiding him to follow the rules, to take things one careful step at a time.

There are no second chances. Life gave no reprieves, Mother warned. Without accuracy, without precision, one could look forward to nothing but stumbling failure. He knew all about failure.

An excruciating pain behind his eye interrupted his grim introspection, and he quickened his pace toward his car. Perhaps he'd left a pair of sunglasses in the glove box.

With his good eye, he swept the sunny perimeter of the cemetery. Deirdre was nowhere to be seen. A panicky feeling rose inside him. He wondered when and where he would see her again. Would she blame him for their quarrel when she spoke with Mother? Would she try to sabotage his next venture? Regret twisted an agonizing knot inside him. Maybe when it was all over, when he and Mother were together again, he could try to explain.

He cast a nervous glance over his shoulder at the blond woman still standing with head bowed across the lawn beside the grave. In some perverse way it pleased him that Deirdre hadn't known how close they'd been to the woman whose name was last on his list.

"But we know, don't we, Kelsey?" he whispered. "The best for last. Isn't that how the old saying goes? And I promise I won't keep you waiting a moment longer than is absolutely necessary."

When he crossed the street, he spotted Deirdre waiting for him at his car. He tried to return her smile, relief flooding him. She wasn't really angry, only playing her old games. With luck, she might not even tell Mother they'd quarreled.

He couldn't afford to let these petty problems with Deirdre distract him, he told himself, not at this late date, not when his grand finale was so close at hand. Through the grinding pain he visualized the woman he would meet tonight. With a surgeon's skill he would execute his plan once more.

As he opened the car door and waited for Deirdre to get in, his mind ticked off every detail, every moment of the days to come. He loved to dwell on the final scene when Mother applauded his hard work, when Deirdre was forced to relinquish control, when he could shake off his *own* false identity at last.

He had followed his plan to the letter with the others, and accomplished complete success. He dared not become overconfident, an inner voice warned. If he took a false step, committed one stupid mistake, there could be no second chance. No reprieve, as Mother had said. For even though there would always be more women, each of them could die only once.

THE MINISTER uttered his final words and closed his bible noiselessly. Somewhere in the back of her mind Kelsey heard the distant noises of the city and the low murmur of the small knot of people gathered around her. She wasn't oblivious to their concerned stares, merely numbed, her conscious mind registering little more than the thudding of her own heart.

Her arms and legs felt leaden, but an inner voice told her it was time to go. Willing her muscles to respond, she placed a single yellow rose on top of the spray of flowers that draped the coffin. Her hand lingered as she closed her eyes and listened to her heart whisper a final goodbye.

In a moment she took a deep breath, opened her eyes and offered her quiet thanks to the minister. Then she turned to the small, stoop-shouldered man beside her. "It's time to go, Cecil," she said softly. He nodded without disturbing a strand of the thin gray hair that lay like wispy threads across his head.

As they walked toward her car, Kelsey saw Vanessa Overholt, the attorney whose services Shannon had retained to carry on the long-distance property battle with Douglas, standing beside a sleek, metallic blue import.

Earlier this afternoon at the church, Kelsey had seen Vanessa and Roger McElroy walk in together. She'd assumed they'd come to the cemetery together, as well.

But Kelsey didn't see Roger now, and she couldn't remember seeing him at the grave, either.

Then again, Kelsey told herself, she'd probably missed many of the details of the emotionally draining afternoon. She could have sworn Nelson Masters had followed her in his car when they'd left the small chapel where the service for Shannon had been held. But when Kelsey arrived at the cemetery, she hadn't seen Nelson, either.

When Shannon's father touched her elbow, it jolted Kelsey out of her thoughts. It took an act of iron will for her to resist shrugging away from his touch. How easy it would be to be angry with Cecil Burrows, Kelsey told herself, to pin all her pain onto such an easy target. But if loss and remorse weighed heavily on her own heart today, Kelsey could only guess at the weight of Cecil's private burden. What must the man who had given his only daughter a lifetime of disappointments be feeling today?

She turned to him when they reached her car. "I guess this is goodbye for now, Cecil," she said. "Are you going to be all right?"

"I'll be okay," he managed, his eyes glistening, his bulbous nose blue-veined and shiny. "It...it was a nice service. The things the preacher said, the flowers and all." He released a labored sigh. "Seems like I should have done more."

Kelsey listened uneasily. How could she find the words of absolution Cecil Burrows was groping for?

"I appreciate everything you've done, Kelsey. I don't know how I can ever repay you—"

She interrupted him with a firm hand on his sleeve. "Please, don't say any more," she pleaded. "It's all right. Shannon was my friend."

"Now that's a fact," he said, nodding vigorously. A shimmering veil of sweat had risen on his forehead and upper lip.

To combat the sting of tears that began to blur her vision, Kelsey began a concentrated search through her purse for her car keys. "Are you planning on staying in Chicago, Cecil?"

"No," he said quickly. "In fact I'm leaving this afternoon for California. Got some shirttail family out there."

Kelsey was secretly relieved. Cecil Burrows's restlessness was unnerving, his constant state of unease making him seem always on the verge of flight.

"You'll see to her . . . things, won't you, Kelsey?"

She swallowed the anguished little cry that rose in her throat. There had been so many other things to think about. It hadn't occurred to her what would be done with Shannon's belongings. "Of course," she assured him, her voice husky.

"I knew I could count on you."

Kelsey's fingers finally closed around her car keys. "Well, I guess this is goodbye, Cecil."

For a moment they stood in awkward silence; both knew they had little else to say to each other. Then without warning Cecil blurted out, "Oh, why did this have to happen, Kelsey?" His eyes glistened as he reached for her arm. His outburst had the effect of an electric shock jolting through Kelsey's nervous system, leaving her temporarily numb and speechless.

"You know, she should have never have divorced." His tone turned accusing and bitter. "Douglas isn't such a bad guy, is he? She always had money. Damn it, she was all I had! And now that she's gone, what the hell am I supposed to do?"

His unabashed selfishness ignited Kelsey's wrath, and she jerked her arm away from his grasp. "Stop it!" she shouted, stunning herself. He recoiled as though she'd slapped him, and for one crazy moment Kelsey half wished she had. She glared at him, her entire body trembling, the tide of emotions building inside her growing dangerously close to washing away the final barriers of her restraint.

"Kelsey?" She hadn't realized that anyone had moved up behind her, but she recognized Ben's voice immediately, and a wave of inexplicable relief washed over her when she whirled around to face him. She hadn't seen him since the wretched day of Shannon's death, but she had talked to him a couple of times on the phone concerning the break-in.

"Tanner," Kelsey said a bit breathlessly.

"Ben," he amended. He wasn't quite smiling, but his expression was friendly and more than a bit disconcerting. Too often in the past couple of days, fleeting images of the tall, rugged police officer had offered Kelsey a disturbing, albeit pleasant, distraction. A distraction she couldn't afford, she warned herself again, even as she noted that his eyes really were the most unusual and interesting shade of gray.

"Mr. Hughes," Ben acknowledged Cecil, his expression somber and sympathetic. Cecil merely nodded. Although earlier Cecil had been quite outspoken to Kelsey in what he'd described as the Chicago Police

Department's halfhearted attempt to track down Shannon's murderer, he seemed to have nothing to say to Ben.

"I didn't see you at the service," Kelsey noted, attempting to fill the uneasy silence.

"I just arrived," Ben explained. His gaze roamed over her face, his expression betraying his concern.

Kelsey looked past Ben, and his eyes followed hers to the sidewalk to take in the couple moving quickly toward them. Vanessa Overholt moved with the easy grace of the confident and successful professional that she was. This afternoon her thick blond hair was pulled into a sleek chignon at her nape. The teal green silk suit she wore fit her lithe figure with tailored perfection.

The man walking beside her provided a startling contrast to Vanessa's sophisticated silhouette. Roger McElroy, a stocky, big-boned man, was an inch or two taller than Vanessa. His dark brown hair was cut military-short on the sides and top. When Kelsey had first been introduced to Roger a little over two years ago, she remembered thinking that Roger's blunt facial features and swaggering demeanor gave him the hard-boiled appearance of a detective straight out of fiction.

Kelsey sometimes wondered if Roger hadn't consciously tried to enhance that image. In the past year she could count the number of times she'd seen him without his rumpled raincoat.

"Tough day, huh, kid?" Roger said, his Mickey Spillane persona firmly in place. She couldn't see his dark eyes behind his sunglasses as he reached for her hand. "You know, if there's anything I can do..." He squeezed her hand to emphasize the sincerity of his offer.

"Thank you," Kelsey said, her voice tight, unnaturally high and strained as she politely extracted her hand from Roger's overly warm grip.

"This is all just so unbelievable." Vanessa's tone and expression were deeply sympathetic as her eyes traveled from Kelsey to Cecil and back again. When she finally settled her gaze on Ben, Kelsey couldn't help but notice the open appreciation glinting in Vanessa's large green eyes.

"Detective Ben Tanner," Kelsey said. "Vanessa Overholt, Shannon's lawyer."

"And friend," Vanessa added, extending her hand. "Nice to meet you, Detective."

"Detective Tanner is the officer assigned to Shannon's case. Ben this is Roger Mc—"

"We've met," Ben put in before she could finish. Kelsey noted a subtle tightening of the muscles in Ben's jawline as he leveled his attention on Roger, whose own response was a curt nod, followed by a stiffening of his spine as though he were trying to achieve his maximum height.

Despite the many thoughts and emotions vying for her attention, Kelsey couldn't help wondering how and when Ben and Roger had met. That the two men had an unspoken animosity was clear. Some previous encounter—an encounter that Kelsey knew instinctively hadn't been a good one—had set the dark tone for this meeting.

"Well, we need to get going. Hey, I'm sorry about this, Kels. I thought a lot of Shannon. She was a good kid," Roger added before turning his attention to Vanessa and giving her an unspoken cue that it was past time for them to leave.

"Mr. Hughes, I'm so sorry for your loss," Vanessa said quietly. "I'll be in touch, Kelsey. We need to tie up some loose ends...." She touched Kelsey's arm and held her eyes meaningfully. *Douglas,* she mouthed, her expression dramatically grim.

Kelsey nodded. "I plan to be back in my office day after tomorrow."

"Perhaps we'll meet again, Detective Tanner," Vanessa said, her tone hopeful.

"Perhaps we will," Ben said.

Kelsey felt Ben's eyes on her as she watched Roger and Vanessa walk away. When she turned back to him she could feel the questions she saw in his eyes and wondered what they were.

"Do you need a lift somewhere, Mr. Hughes?" Ben asked Cecil.

"Yeah, as a matter of fact I was just about to ask Kelsey to drive me to the bus station," Cecil replied.

Before she had time to respond, Ben said, "I'm headed that way now. I'll drive you." The edge of authority in his voice didn't welcome discussion.

Kelsey felt like hugging Ben. The mere thought of spending another minute with Cecil Burrows seemed suddenly intolerable.

"That's my car," Ben said, indicating the dark green two-door parked a couple of spaces behind Kelsey's. He handed Cecil the keys. "I'll be right over."

Cecil quickly said goodbye to Kelsey and hurried over to Ben's car. "Thanks," she murmured once she was sure Cecil was out of earshot. "How did you know?"

"Just a guess."

"And a bit of eavesdropping?"

"Comes with the territory, I'm afraid."

She nodded. "I know what you mean. It can be habit-forming, can't it?" She slid her car keys into the lock, opened the door and slipped behind the wheel. The air swirling inside the Chevy felt as if it came from a blast furnace.

"After I drop Cecil off, I'd like to come by and see you. Would you be up to some company later?" he asked leaning into the doorway, one hand on the door and the other on the roof as Kelsey rolled down her window.

"I don't know. Maybe. Would *you* be up to answering some questions?"

His brows drew together in a dark line, hooding his smoky gaze and making it difficult for her to read his expression.

"You haven't forgotten that you promised to include me in your investigation, have you, Detective Tanner?"

"I haven't forgotten, but I wish you'd drop the formalities. Whenever I hear someone say Detective Tanner, I start looking over my shoulder for my old man."

"No kidding? You too?"

"Second-generation public servant at your service."

Kelsey smiled. Their light banter had been precisely what she'd needed. Despite the circumstances and their surroundings, her smile was the first real one she'd felt in days.

"So how about it? We still have a lot to talk about."

"We do," she agreed. "But right now I need time alone." The task that awaited her at Shannon's apartment erased her smile. "Cecil asked me to see to Shannon's belongings."

The tightness around his eyes returned. "Can't it wait?"

Kelsey shook her head as she turned the keys in the ignition and gunned the Chevy to life, fiddling with the switch on the broken air conditioner, praying for cool air.

"Then let me help you," he said. "I'll come by later and we'll drive over together."

"But why?"

He studied her face for a moment. "Seeing the apartment again will give me a chance to take a closer look, to see if the lab might have overlooked anything, any evidence that might give us a new lead."

She eyed him skeptically. Everything she knew about him so far told her he was the kind of man who did things right the first time. From her father she'd picked up enough information about police procedure to know that a man as relatively young as Ben didn't rise to the position of homicide detective by waiting three days to assess a crime scene.

"Come on, Kelsey," he prodded when she didn't answer. "I have the evening off. If you insist on taking care of this today, at least let me help."

Common sense warned her to resist his offer, but at the moment she didn't seem to know why. Besides, just hearing the words *evidence* and *leads* reminded her that finding Shannon's killer was really their only mutual objective.

"Fine," she agreed.

"Are you sure you're up to this?" he asked. "Are you going to be all right?"

She could only nod, wondering how she could begin to explain to this man, who despite her frivolous fantasies was still a virtual stranger, that at the moment it seemed impossible that anything would ever be all right again. But a moment later, when he reached for her hand, he seemed to be communicating that he already understood everything completely.

"I'll come by your place and pick you up after I drop Cecil off at the bus station."

She nodded.

"You'll wait for me, then?"

"I will," she said, although making any kind of promise to this confident cop with the steel gray eyes made her feel as though she were stepping out onto a shaky ledge, staring down from some dizzying height. Definitely not a safe place for a lady to be, Kelsey's inner voice warned. "But I really don't see why we can't just meet at the apartment."

He arched one eyebrow and smiled. "Well, for one thing my air conditioner isn't broken."

"Good point," she conceded, as she pulled a pen out of her purse and wrote down her address on the back of her business card. "I still have a lot of questions for you, Detective Tanner."

His fingertips grazed hers as he accepted the paper she held out to him. "I still have a lot of questions of my own," he said evenly. "Who knows? Maybe later this evening we'll both find what we're looking for."

His attitude of optimism caused the awful weight that had been pressing down on her for the past three days to shift. His steady confidence and ready reassurances comforted her, attracted her. But it was an attraction that scared her, an attraction she wasn't at all sure she was prepared to feel. After all, he *is* a cop, she reminded herself.

But even as she watched him walk away, she let herself indulge in a fantasy of what it might be like if he wasn't.

Kelsey turned on the radio as she pulled away from the curb, hoping to banish her dangerous daydreams with the music. But a block later she knew she had failed as unreasonable disappointment settled over her when she allowed herself a peek into the rearview mirror and discovered that Ben's car was no longer behind hers.

Come on, Kelsey, she scolded herself. What's the matter with you? Don't you know by now there's never a cop around when you really need one?

Chapter Four

Half an hour later, Ben watched from his car to make sure Cecil Burrows had boarded the bus bound for Los Angeles. Under different circumstances Shannon Hughes's father might just as easily have been headed for jail, Ben told himself as he watched Cecil climb onto the bus.

When the two uniformed policemen had arrived last night and found Cecil trying to break into his daughter's Lakeview apartment, they weren't in the mood for excuses. Luckily for Cecil, Ben had heard the call come in and recognized the address. Curiosity had driven him to respond.

In light of the circumstances, Ben doubted if Cecil would have been taken into custody—even the most jaded Chicago beat cop would have hesitated to press the issue once Cecil explained that the apartment had been his deceased daughter's. But the building manager hadn't been so easily mollified, and Ben had had to do a bit of talking to persuade her not to press charges for the damage Cecil had done to the door.

Ben winced, remembering how once inside the apartment, Cecil had proceeded to rummage through his daughter's belongings, searching frantically for something he wouldn't name. Legalities aside, Cecil's actions had been appalling and reprehensible. With a father like Cecil Burrows, Ben told himself, it was no wonder Shannon Hughes had had a rough life.

When he'd arrived on the scene last night, Ben assessed the situation and immediately took over, dismissing the two patrolmen who had arrived before him. The fact that Cecil was trying to convince the apartment manager to contact Kelsey St. James to come and vouch for him prompted Ben to act with even greater dispatch. The last thing Kelsey needed on the night before her best friend's funeral was to contend with Shannon's drunken father.

Despite his aversion to dealing with Cecil, Ben had taken the old man to an all-night coffee shop and sobered him up. It was after three when Cecil finally admitted the reason he'd been desperate to get into his daughter's apartment.

Ben found he could dredge up little sympathy when Cecil confessed to his indebtedness to a local loan shark. Once the old man broke down, he filled Ben in on all the sordid details. Ben hadn't needed a medical degree to diagnose the old man's problem—Cecil Burrows was as addicted to gambling as some men were to hard drugs.

According to what Cecil said, Shannon had agreed to give him the money he needed to pay off the loan shark on condition that he get help for his drinking and gambling problems. "I made her that promise," Cecil had said, "just two days before she was killed. I was supposed to pick up the money on Saturday."

Cecil had gone on to explain how he'd tried to lie low until Shannon could raise the money, but a couple of the loan shark's men had found him. "They threatened to break both my legs!" Cecil had revealed. Finally, he'd been able to persuade them to give him more time. But then Shannon was killed. "I'm finished!" Cecil had cried. "Don't you see, if I don't get my hands on that money, I'm as good as dead."

Ben remembered how the old man's spirits had suddenly brightened when his thoughts came round again to Kelsey. She would know what to do, Cecil had insisted. Shannon told Kelsey everything. She might even know what Shannon had done with the money she'd promised to give him.

Ben's hand had closed around Cecil's arm like a vise when he'd tried to go call Kelsey. It was then that he'd given Cecil his options: protection for the next twenty-four hours and a one-way ticket out of town, or immediate arrest on the charges of breaking and entering and illegal gambling.

The look on Cecil's face made it unnecessary for Ben to check for a past criminal record. It was obvious that the old man had served time before, and he had no desire to go back.

Ben had handed Cecil's signed statement, naming his bookie and several of his associates, over to vice within the hour. Unfortunately Cecil swore he'd never known the loan shark's name, that he'd merely been given a phone number and an address where and date when to pick up the money. He also claimed just as adamantly that he knew nothing about the break-in at Kelsey's office. Based on Cecil's amateurish attempts to break into his daughter's apartment, Ben's decision was to accept Cecil's claim of innocence. At least for the time being.

But whether Cecil had been telling the truth when he claimed not to know the identity of the loan shark, Ben still wasn't sure. Cecil feared the loan shark more than he feared jail. Privately, Ben had to admit it was a reasonable fear.

By 7:00 a.m., three of the bookie's closest associates had been brought in for questioning. With luck, Ben told himself as he signaled for the Lakeview exit, one of them would bargain himself out of trouble and his boss into an iron-clad case for the prosecution.

It had been a long night and a hectic day. Ben was reminded of just how long by the fatigue burning between his shoulder blades as his eyes swept the tree-lined avenue for Kelsey's street. It hadn't been a bad night's work, though: Cecil Burrows had been given a reprieve and was safely on his way out of town, a couple more criminals had been removed from Chicago's streets and with luck one less bookie would be in operation by nightfall. Not bad for a short twelve-hour span, Ben told himself. But he was far from satisfied.

A loan shark with the means and muscle to extort money and terrify poor slobs like Cecil Burrows was still in full operation and a clever thief who had burgled St. James Investigations was still at large. But worst of all, a young woman who should still be alive wasn't.

And the connection between these three situations—Ben's gut told him there had to be a connection—was still unknown.

He spotted the small white-framed bungalow at the address Kelsey had written on the back of her card. But when he pulled up to the curb and shut off the engine, he still felt he had a long, long way to go.

"YOU'RE EARLY," she said, opening the door and motioning him inside. Ben followed her quick movements down a narrow hallway and through an arched entry into an airy kitchen. Following Kelsey anywhere in those softly faded, snug-fitting blue jeans would be a pleasure, he admitted to himself as he stood in the doorway, watching her retrieve a large bag of dog food from the cupboard under the sink.

Drawn by the rustling sound of the bag, a large, keen-eyed collie brushed past him. With a look of open adoration, the dog pranced around Kelsey's feet as she lifted the bag over the stainless steel dish on the countertop. Ben saw the contents of the bag begin to shift, and in two quick steps he was beside her, his hands splayed over hers as he helped tip the bag back before dog food rained down over the counter and onto the floor.

The fresh scent of her perfume teased at his nose. The warmth of her sweet breath felt good on his face. The flush of color that rose on her cheeks and her slightly nervous smile made his pulse quicken. Ben had met a lot of PI's in his time. He'd even gone so far as to trust one or two. But never in fifteen years on the force had he wanted to kiss one the way he longed to kiss Kelsey St. James now. He eased the bag out of her hands.

"Thanks," she murmured, avoiding his eyes with a flutter of thick, golden lashes that told him she was just as aware as he of the chemistry that had been simmering between them from the moment they'd met.

But right now it was forty pounds of impatient dog that edged in between them. "Hold on, boy," Ben said as he finished filling the bowl.

"This is Sherlock," she said as she set the bowl down onto a small braided rug with one hand and patted the dog affectionately with the other.

"He's a beauty," Ben said, stroking the dog's head. "This is a nice place," he added, surveying the kitchen and the adjoining dining room.

"I was lucky to find it," she explained. "We needed a yard."

"Charlie Chan, Sherlock...hmmm. I think I detect a pattern," he said. "By the way, how is Mr. Chan?"

He found her sudden smile a stunning surprise that sent a wave of heat rippling through him.

"I'm afraid he's still pouting," she replied playfully. "Hasn't spoken to me since I brought him home from the vet's."

Ben's burst of laughter set off a flurry of movement and the sound of paws skittering across the polished wood floor in the dining room. "What was that?" he asked as a blur of black and white rounded the corner and disappeared into the living room.

"That would be Miss Marple and Dolly. They're shy around strangers, especially Dolly." Kelsey bent down on one knee. A white kitten with huge blue eyes peeped tentatively from behind the couch. Kelsey coaxed her, "Come on, Dolly. Come on, sweetheart. No one is going to hurt you."

Keeping one suspicious eye trained on Ben, the kitten, who was no more than a ball of snowy fur, crept cautiously toward Kelsey, keeping her body stiff and ready to spring should Ben make a false move.

"Good girl," Kelsey said as the kitten finally tip-toed up onto her lap and immediately rolled over. "She loves to have her tummy rubbed." Kelsey smiled.

"Miss Marple, Sherlock, Charlie Chan," he said. "Tell me, how did a delicate little thing like Dolly manage to wind up in the company of these hard-boiled and infamous sleuths?"

With regret, Ben watched the smile fade from Kelsey's pretty face and the soft lights dim in her eyes. She set the kitten down on the kitchen floor, where it proceeded to hunch its back and hiss at him before scampering back to its hiding place.

"Someone else named Dolly," she said quietly, diverting her attention to straightening a dish towel that hung on a metal bar beside the sink. "Ready?" she asked, and without waiting for him to reply she snatched her small leather purse from the counter and headed for the back door. "We can go out this way."

He followed her again as she opened the door and stepped out onto a small covered patio where several empty cardboard boxes were stacked. Ben glanced at his watch. The air felt as thick and hot as it had at noon, yet it was already half past five.

"I thought we might need these," she explained. "I've arranged for movers to haul the furniture to a month-to-month storage unit until I can figure out where it all should go, but tonight I want to bring some of her more... personal things home with me."

Together they gathered the boxes and carried them with them as they walked around the side of the house.

Kelsey was silent until they'd finished loading the boxes into the trunk of Ben's car.

When he slammed the trunk closed, Kelsey leaned against the back of the car and folded her arms in front of her. Her eyes seemed to focus on something in the distance that only she could see.

"Three weeks ago I gave Dolly to Shannon as a housewarming present," she said softly. "The kitten came from the shelter—all my animals came from there, with the exception of Mr. Chan." Her quick smile didn't quite reach her eyes. "Charlie just pranced through my back door one day, half starved, carrying scars from his latest battle like medals of honor. I guess you could say *he* chose *me* to rescue him." Ben found her dry, throaty chuckle incredibly appealing.

"Anyway, I picked up Dolly on my way home from the cemetery today. Mrs. Vaughn, the manager at Shannon's building, had been keeping an eye on her for me." She stared at him as though she expected him to start explaining. Ben pretended not to notice.

If she had spoken with the apartment manager this afternoon, chances were good she knew about the bizarre events that had taken place at Shannon's apartment last night. Ben wondered when the questions would begin, but then he reminded himself that if Kelsey had been aware of Cecil's financial dilemma, some of those questions might be unnecessary.

When Ben didn't say anything, Kelsey went on to explain how Mrs. Vaughn had been able to lure the frightened kitten into her apartment. Ben tried to concentrate on what she was saying, but he found himself distracted by the way the sunlight sent tiny explosions of gold highlights dancing through her hair every time she moved her head.

"Dolly was still cowering in a corner when I picked her up," she said.

"Are you going to keep her?"

"Of course. Dolly is skittish, and she doesn't trust strangers—especially men. But once you win her over, she's a real little love."

Ben couldn't help making a mental comparison between Kelsey and the defensive little creature he'd encountered inside the house. Like Dolly's hissing and arching, perhaps Kelsey's bravado was merely a show to mask her fears, as well.

As she walked around to the passenger side of the car, Ben wondered when the next shoe would drop. He didn't have to wonder long. Once they were both inside the car, she turned in her seat and trained her gaze squarely on his. "Mrs. Vaughn told me about last night, Tanner. She said she called the police and that you showed up and hauled Cecil away."

"That's right, I did."

"Well, what happened?"

"It's a long story."

"I've got lots of time."

He matched her scrutiny in silence, studying the determined tilt of her chin, the intelligent light in her soft blue eyes, the gentle upturn of her nose. Every instinct shouted for him to believe that a woman as lovely and as obviously caring and decent as Kelsey St. James couldn't possibly be involved with the likes of Roger McElroy. His smile was involuntary, but it faded when met with her stony glare.

"You promised me some answers, Tanner," she reminded him, the edge of irritation in her voice surprisingly rough.

"I haven't forgotten," he said as he turned the key in the ignition.

"Good. Now, why don't you start explaining just what the hell happened last night?" she demanded, reminding Ben that this was one kitten who wouldn't hesitate to show her claws.

THE DRIVE between Kelsey's house and the Lakeview apartment building that had been Shannon Hughes's last home took less than ten minutes. But as Ben found himself the target of Kelsey's constant questions, he started wishing the distance was even shorter.

"Do you mean to tell me that Cecil tried to break into his own daughter's apartment?" He sensed her inner shudder.

"It sure looked that way," he said. "He'd been drinking and he was pretty emotional."

"Good Lord," Kelsey muttered, shaking her head. "Why didn't he call me? I had the key. I would have let him in, talked to him, tried to help."

Ben felt an inner reaction of his own, remembering how close Cecil had come to doing just that, calling Kelsey and dragging her into the middle of the whole sordid situation. Like the stray animals that wandered into her life seeking refuge, Cecil Burrows could have easily become Kelsey's next mission of mercy, Ben suspected.

"I guess he wasn't thinking straight," he said, realizing with no small measure of discomfort that somewhere along the line he'd decided that Kelsey St. James needed his personal protection.

"What could he have wanted so badly that it couldn't have waited until he saw me today at the service? Do you know what he was looking for? Did he say?"

"Like I said before," Ben hedged, "he wasn't making a whole lot of sense."

As they pulled up in front of the apartment building and Ben reached to open his door, Kelsey stopped him with a hand on his arm. "This is all about money, isn't it?" she asked. She didn't give him time to respond before she added, "I should have known. He must have been really desperate this time."

Ben felt the muscles in his face tighten and realized he hoped an admission of her knowledge of Cecil's gambling activities was not forthcoming. If she knew about his gambling, it was all too likely that she knew about the loan shark. "Why do you say that?" he asked.

"Cecil was always desperate," she said quickly. "Always trying to cover his bets."

"What do you know, Kelsey?" he prodded. "Tell me what you know about Cecil's money problems."

He saw her wince at what had sounded, even to his own ears, too much like an official interrogation.

"I know that he gambled, and that he seldom won," she answered.

"And?"

She shrugged and he felt a wave of dark disappointment wash through him. She knew more, a lot more, and this time it was his turn to prevent her from getting out of the car. The lady was bright, tough and obviously clever. Perhaps in the end he would be the one who wound up needing protection.

She glared down at his hand on her arm. "Oh, all right," she conceded. "Shannon told me her father was in trouble."

"What do you know about this trouble?"

Ben watched her make the decision to lie.

"Not much except that Shannon was going to bail him out again," she murmured, her eyes falling away from his as she reached again for the door.

"You'd make a lousy poker player, Kelsey."

She didn't look at him, but her hand froze on the door handle for an instant before she jerked it open and stepped out onto the sidewalk.

Ben walked around to the back of the car and she moved up beside him as he opened the trunk.

"Cecil must have been frantic," she said quietly.

He turned to face her. "He was."

"I begged Shannon to go to the police when she told me about the loan shark, but she didn't want to implicate her father."

He knew he ought to remind her that as a licensed private investigator with the State of Illinois she had an implied obligation to report the kind of criminal activity she suspected Cecil might be involved in. But he decided to save the lecture. Sometime in the past five minutes she'd decided to start trusting him, and Ben had no intention of shattering that fragile beginning by reminding her of their professional differences.

Her expression was solemn when she said, "Last weekend Shannon told me she still hadn't raised all the cash her father needed. What else could I do but loan her the difference? She said he'd promised her it would never happen again.''

He felt the same anger toward Cecil that he saw flickering in Kelsey's eyes. Ben hadn't known Shannon Hughes, but he'd known too many guys like Cecil. Any daughter deserved better from her father.

"Where is Cecil now?" she asked. "In protective custody? You know he won't be safe anywhere in Chicago until he comes up with that money."

"I know. That's why he's on his way to parts unknown."

"California."

Damn it, Cecil had sworn he hadn't told anyone where he was going. Ben wondered now if, for everyone's sake, he'd have been wiser to lock the old man up and force him to swallow the key. The last person Ben wanted to see dragged into Cecil's dilemma was Kelsey, but obviously she didn't see the danger. In fact, she seemed strangely relieved.

"I guess I just assumed that Cecil had paid the money and that it was all over. Now I guess it really is. I'm glad Cecil is safe. I just hope he's finally learned his lesson."

"Why do you assume it's over?" he asked.

"Well, isn't it? When you guys want someone to disappear, they disappear, right?"

"Cecil didn't enter a witness protection program, Kelsey. He got a free bus ride out of town and little more. The kind of people who'll be looking for him have some very long tentacles. If he keeps his nose clean, he'll probably be all right. He can make a fresh start. But with his track record, I can't help but wonder how long it will take him to find a new bookie."

Kelsey's expression grew grim. "And the kind of people Cecil was dealing with aren't exactly the forgiving types, are they?"

He shook his head.

"Oh, my God, Ben," she gasped. "You don't think the loan shark came after Shannon, do you?" He could almost hear her mind fitting the gruesome pieces in place.

"I don't think we can afford to rule out anything at this point."

They unloaded the rest of the boxes in silence. The implication of Shannon Hughes's involvement with her father's illegal dealings presented itself to Ben as he worked. Shannon's death could have been meant as a deadly warning to her father, an example to those pathetic souls who had the misfortune to still owe money to the loan shark.

It was a grim scenario, one that made Ben's blood churn with anger. But until the investigation of Shannon's death was thoroughly investigated and Cecil's mysterious loan shark arrested, Ben knew better than to second-guess.

The investigation he intended to conduct would be thorough and exacting, every piece of evidence would be examined and reexamined. The coroner's report that he could picture still sitting on his desk would be read and reread. And tonight, before Ben left Lakeview, he hoped to view the scene of the crime with fresh eyes.

If even the barest shred of evidence told him Shannon Hughes's death was linked to organized crime, Ben promised himself he would yank Kelsey St. James's private investigator's license without blinking an eye.

She wasn't prepared for this kind of case. He remembered the details of the background check he'd run on St. James Investigations this morning. Insurance fraud, workers' compensation claims and a handful of missing person investigations had comprised the bulk of Kelsey's business over the past three years. As far as Ben could tell, she had neither the experience not the savvy to handle a full-blown criminal investigation. And he wasn't about to sit back and watch her cut her professional teeth on this one, especially in light of her personal involvement.

That kind of personal interest caused one to make stupid mistakes, take stupid chances. Ben knew firsthand that guys like the ones who had threatened Cecil and possibly killed his daughter didn't give second chances.

Ben followed Kelsey into the apartment building, and as they began stacking boxes into the elevator, he felt as though he'd personally ushered her into the vortex of a deadly storm. The only way he could rationalize his promise of a shared investigation was his private vow to usher her right back out as soon as possible.

But something told him it wouldn't be that easy. In the end, solving the mystery of Shannon Hughes's death and putting a Chicago loan shark out of business might prove simpler than extracting one very pretty, very stubborn female PI from the middle of a murder investigation.

Chapter Five

The moment she opened the door, Kelsey knew she wasn't prepared for what she saw. Shannon's apartment was clean and neat, the way she'd always kept it. Not a throw pillow or a magazine out of place. The pendulum suspended beneath the moon-faced clock on the wall above the couch ticked off the moments with unerring reliability. The philodendron and the spider plants on the windowsill were thriving. And yet the air was charged with expectancy, as if at any moment Shannon would breeze into the living room and offer them a drink or something to eat. Kelsey held her breath and when she realized what she was waiting for, a fresh ache settled in her heart.

Whatever she'd expected to see or feel in the place where Shannon had lived out the last few precious moments of her life, this mocking facade of normalcy was exactly what Kelsey hadn't been prepared to face.

With Ben close behind her, she stepped into the apartment. The moment he shut the door behind them, she felt the blood draining from her face. The floor seemed to tilt. She reached for the back of the couch for support.

"I'm not sure this is such a good idea," Ben said as he moved up beside her and placed his hand gently at the small of her back. "Are you going to be okay? Do you want to leave?"

Kelsey shook her head. She was glad he was with her. "I'll be fine," she lied. "It's the altitude." His eyes followed hers to the French doors at the opposite end of the living room. "I feel safer on the ground, that's all."

He studied her face and she knew he was trying to decide whether to force the issue of leaving. "We can look over the apartment, pack up the things you want to take with you and leave. The lab went over the balcony area with a fine-tooth comb," he said. "There's no reason for you to go out there, Kelsey."

"I'm an investigator," she reminded him as much for her own benefit as his. "Shannon was pushed to her death from that balcony." The scene of the crime, she added to herself morosely. "This is something I have to do," she said softly, hoping he'd understand and not try to stop her.

He walked with her as she moved steadily toward the French doors that opened out onto the balcony.

"You really don't have to do this," he said again. "You don't have to prove anything, you know." His low voice resonated his concern, a stark contrast to the words from the past that echoed through her mind.

"Just like her mother," her father had stated loudly to the crowd of Kelsey's classmates waiting in line at the Ferris wheel, *"afraid of her own shadow."* When Kelsey closed her eyes, she could see her father's scowling face glaring down at her as the Ferris wheel swayed to life and lifted him up into the evening sky,

leaving his humiliated and trembling eight-year-old daughter below. "Face your fears, Kelsey," he'd lectured on the way home that night. "Learn to face up to them or you might as well stop living."

The bitterness that accompanied her memories sparked the old resentment and fueled her resolve. "I have to do this," she said, praying all the while Ben Tanner would never know how hard she had to fight the impulse to throw herself into his arms and beg him to get her the hell out of there.

"Give me your hand," he said, stunning her with his simple request.

"Don't be silly." Her words tumbled out in a breathless rush.

"Come on, Kelsey. Just take my hand."

She stared at him, assessing his sincerity. His somber expression assured her that he was serious. As he reached for her hand, a tiny flutter in her chest told Kelsey that this unpredictable, hopelessly disarming cop had chipped another chink in the armor that protected her heart.

As his hand closed around hers, the words of gratitude froze in her throat. She wondered if she would ever be able to express how much his kindness, his gentle understanding meant to her.

"Here goes," she whispered finally, exhaling a shaky breath as she reached for the door and turned the knob.

The rush of humid air, blended with the muted sounds of traffic ten floors below, kicked up a maelstrom of physical and emotional reactions inside her. Kelsey struggled to maintain her poise.

Somehow it seemed Ben sensed her inner turmoil and he tightened his grip on her hand. "I'm right here," he reminded her softly. "I won't let go, Kelsey."

Clutching his promise to her heart, she found the strength to step out onto the balcony. *Take it easy,* she ordered herself. *One step at a time. Take a look around. Look at the planks on the floor, at the red geraniums in the corner. Look anywhere but down. Just don't look down, Kelsey,* she warned herself, *and you'll survive this.*

Her eyes focused on the corner of waist-high railing where it butted up against the side of the brick building. Cautiously she allowed her gaze to travel the length of the railing, being careful to keep her gaze from wandering to the void below.

With a trembling hand, she reached out to touch the railing, hesitating only a second before her fingers touched wood.

"It's all right," he assured her. "It's already been dusted for prints."

With emotion welling in her chest like an overinflated balloon, her fingers clutched the wood as she forced herself to look at the jagged break in the redwood where the railing had given way. At that instant a horn blast from a car below startled the air. Kelsey gasped and glanced down.

Barely managing to stifle her scream, she stumbled backward. A cascade of suffocating images smothered her: Shannon standing on the balcony pressed against the railing, the sickening sound of wood splitting, a breathless moment of hesitation and then the terrifying, timeless fall.

Kelsey's heart was a jackhammer against her chest. Her stomach lurched. As the horrifying scenes her imagination had conjured appeared in vivid detail in her mind, her knees weakened. Her lungs screamed for air, as a fresh wave of dizziness swept over her.

She heard a faint whimper and somewhere at the edge of her consciousness she realized the cry came from within. Her eyes fluttered closed when the next black wave of vertigo slammed into her.

"No!" she gasped, but the deafening roar of darkness drowned out all sound as it enveloped her, blurring all other sensations and plunging her into mindless and blessed oblivion.

GRADUALLY, through the gauzy veil of that shadowy nightmare, Kelsey realized she was not alone. The memory of the arms that had closed around her somehow managed to seep through to her rational mind, giving her the courage to emerge from the swirling darkness.

She opened her eyes, and the face that she saw hovering above hers was a strong one. The eyes gentle. A shaky breath escaped her lips and the iron bands that squeezed her lungs seemed to melt away. He touched her cheek and the warmth of his smile rippled through her, reassuring her in a way she'd never been comforted before.

Dragging her eyes from his face to study her surroundings, Kelsey realized that she was in Shannon's apartment, lying on Shannon's couch.

"What happened?" she managed, her voice a raspy whisper.

"You checked out on me for a little while," he said.

"I fainted?" she muttered miserably.

He nodded, his expression sympathetic. "It happens," he said simply.

"But not to me," she groaned. Kelsey had had difficulty with heights all her life, but never had she experienced a reaction so extreme.

She tried to sit up but his firm hand on her shoulder and the Chicago Symphony Orchestra's percussion section warming up behind her eyes convinced her otherwise.

"Stay put," he ordered. "I'll get you something cool to drink."

She obeyed, sinking back into the cushions and pulling the cool washcloth that rested on her forehead down over her eyes. The French doors were still open, but despite the warm air that filled the room, she still felt clammy and slightly chilled—not at all up to an argument. "There should be some sodas in the refrigerator," she murmured.

"Diet cola, right?" he called out from the kitchen.

"Nothing escapes that investigator's eye, huh, Tanner?" The lightness in her voice was forced, but she really was pleased that he'd remembered.

"Some would say that," he admitted. "But a compliment from another investigator is always welcome, Ms. St. James."

Kelsey smiled, the warmth of his voice, the gentleness of his tone soothing her jangled senses like a healing balm.

As he moved into the living room, she heard the clinking of glasses and ice and a whoosh when he opened the can of soda. Carefully she scooted to a sitting position and drew her legs up to her chest and wrapped her arms around them. He sat down beside her, draping his arm over the back of the couch and turning so that he faced her.

"What happened out there?" he asked as he handed her a glass.

Before answering, she took a small sip of the cool, bubbly liquid. "It was almost like I could see . . . like I knew how she felt when she fell." Her voice was vapor thin. "The last thing I remember was the sensation that it was me, that I was the one who was falling. That must have been when I blacked out."

He didn't say anything, but he inched closer to her and placed his fingertips on both sides of her face at her temples. At first she tensed when he began making light circular motions with his fingertips. "Relax," he instructed. And with each rhythmic movement, Kelsey felt herself doing just that, relaxing as the pain subsided.

"Where did you learn to do that?" she asked, letting her lids drift closed as she concentrated on his curative touch.

"Just a little something they taught us at detective school."

She opened her eyes and returned his wry smile, deciding that whatever school Detective Ben Tanner had attended, he must have graduated with honors.

Fifteen minutes later, Kelsey's headache was gone and within an hour, she and Ben had all but finished wrapping and packing the fragile items in the kitchen and dining room that Kelsey didn't want to trust to the movers.

After she finished marking yet another box Fragile, she handed it to Ben, and he stacked it beside the door with the others. As he worked, her eyes lingered on his athletic frame for a moment. She was glad he was here. Ben was intelligent, understanding and kind. Beneath that tough, Chicago-cop exterior, Kelsey guessed there was a warm and sensitive individual—a man with whom she wouldn't mind spending more time, getting to know better. Much better, she admitted.

But these weren't normal circumstances, she warned herself. And Ben Tanner was still a cop, a cop with an attitude about private investigators that wasn't a positive one. And packing and lifting boxes wasn't the reason she'd agreed to let him come with her tonight.

He'd promised to let her in on the details of Shannon's case, but not since they'd spoken earlier today at the cemetery had he mentioned any evidence or leads. Somehow Kelsey felt he was waiting for her cue. She decided to end his wait.

"Let's take a break," she said. "I think it's time we talked." She sank down into a dining room chair. He sat down beside her.

"Okay," he said. "Fire when ready."

The man didn't pull any punches, Kelsey noted with an odd mixture of relief and apprehension. "Have you talked to the kids who were in the alley Thursday night?" she asked, fighting the quaver in her voice.

"No, not personally, but I have their revised statements. Seems they didn't actually see Shannon fall, but arrived just moments after. There was a man bending over her when the kids arrived. According to what they saw, it looked as though he was trying to revive her."

Kelsey's thoughts raced, a dozen questions giving birth to a dozen more. "Who was he? Did the ambulance attendants or the police get his name?"

Ben shook his head. "There was no one in the alley when the ambulance arrived."

"Then we've got to talk to those kids again," Kelsey insisted, rising quickly and pacing a few steps into the kitchen. "Perhaps our good Samaritan saw something... or heard something. Maybe he even saw... who pushed her."

"Maybe," he said. "But it's a long shot. According to the coroner, Shannon died around midnight. Lakeview isn't exactly a high crime area, but even so the chances that someone would be strolling down a darkened alley at midnight are slim."

"Then where did he come from?" she asked, and without giving him time to reply she answered her own question. "From the building next door, maybe? Or maybe even from this building. Maybe he's a light sleeper, or maybe he heard something that woke him and he decided to go investigate."

"Maybe," Ben said again. "But no one came forward when the police questioned Shannon's neighbors on Thursday night."

"We need to find that man," Kelsey said vaguely, almost to herself. "He might have been the last person to see Shannon alive." And if for no other reason than that, Kelsey decided she must focus her attention on finding the mystery man in the alley. But where to begin? The weight of that question and the accumulated stress of the day pressed down on Kelsey's heart and she released a labored sigh.

"Maybe we should call it quits," Ben suggested. "You must be tired, and besides, we're almost out of boxes."

Kelsey shook her head, letting her gaze sweep the living room, taking in the knickknacks and photographs Shannon had so recently used to personalize the small apartment.

"There are still quite a few things I want to pack," she explained. The student movers she'd contacted might have had the best rates in town, but she didn't feel like trusting them with items that had held a special place in Shannon's heart.

"I'd hoped to finish up tonight," she explained. Kelsey knew that once she left Shannon's apartment, it wouldn't be easy to force herself to come back again.

"I understand," he said, and the way he said it made her believe that he really did. "We passed a liquor store on the way over," he said. "I'll drive over there and see if I can get some more boxes."

She nodded her thanks.

"Will you be all right?"

"Of course," she assured him. Although she'd been grateful for his presence more than once tonight, Kelsey welcomed these few moments alone. She'd been avoiding going into Shannon's bedroom, afraid of how she might react to the sight of her friend's most personal items, the things that Shannon had held most dear, those things that could only emphasize Kelsey's own loss.

THE BIG MAN in the alleyway slipped into the shadows when he saw the cop emerge from the apartment building, get into his car and drive away. He was sure it was the same cop who had driven off with Cecil Burrows last night, the same cop he'd seen speaking to Kelsey earlier today at the cemetery. He loathed taking care of this kind of thing personally; that's why he'd always paid good money in the past for the services of a small group of flunkies—his "gofers," Shannon had called them.

For a moment his apprehension made him feel weak, but he remembered the gun strapped beneath his vest and he felt stronger. Confronting Kelsey St. James wouldn't be pleasant, but the alternative was worse. He wasn't a man who could survive life in a state penitentiary.

"Damn," he muttered under his breath. The cop could mean real trouble, at best an inconvenience, a complication, an obstacle that must be avoided, worked around or perhaps, in the end, eliminated.

Well, so be it, he told himself as he slipped into the building. In for a dime, in for a dollar, he thought as he stepped into the elevator and punched the button for the tenth floor.

The doors closed, giving him the feeling of being boxed in, trapped, suffocated. *Keep calm,* he admonished himself. *It's almost over.*

If Kelsey cooperated, he could get what he came for and disappear forever. If not . . . well, he couldn't contemplate the situation further. She would cooperate. One way or another he'd have to make sure that she did.

He hated Shannon for pushing him into this, for forcing the situation. He would always hate her and he detested her for the desperation he felt. There was only one way out of this damn mess, and with or without Kelsey St. James's cooperation, Douglas Hughes intended to take it.

SHE HAD JUST FINISHED sorting through the dresser and was perched on the edge of the bed leafing through an old high school yearbook when she heard the apartment door open.

"I'm in here," she called out. "Did you have any luck finding more boxes?"

When Ben didn't answer, Kelsey slid the yearbook off her lap and stood up. "Ben?" she called out tentatively. "Did you—"

Her question was cut short by the appearance of a tree-size man, dressed in an expensive three-piece suit, standing in the doorway.

"Douglas!" she gasped, unconsciously taking a few steps backward. "What are you doing here?"

"I might ask you the same thing, Kelsey," he shot back.

"Cecil had to leave town. He asked me to sort through Shannon's things. The movers are coming tomorrow."

Douglas assessed her coolly, with eyes deep set in his large ruddy face. "Looks like I've come just in time, then," he said, as his gaze swept past her, surveying the room critically.

Kelsey stood up straighter, trying to regain the composure his sudden appearance had shaken. "I'll ask you again, Douglas. What are you doing here?"

"You always were the pushy one, weren't you, Kelsey?" he noted, brushing past her toward the large walk-in closet in the corner of the room.

"Just what do you think you're doing?" she demanded, coming up behind him and grabbing his arm as he shoved the clothes hanging on the rod savagely toward one end of the closet. He shrugged away from her grasp and continued to search through the contents of the closet. When he spotted the polished cedar chest at the foot of Shannon's bed, he crossed over to it and flipped the lid open.

"You have no right to be here," she informed him, her voice icy with contempt as she watched him rummaging through Shannon's personal belongings. Why hadn't she gone with Ben, or at least thought to lock the door after he'd left?

"I have every right," Douglas growled. "Just stay out of my way, Kelsey," he warned. "Let me take what I came for and you won't get hurt."

She'd always known Douglas was a bully, but his blatant threat shocked her. "Get out," she demanded, "before I call the police."

He possessed surprising speed for a man of his size, and when he whirled around and grabbed her upper arm, Kelsey was momentarily too stunned to react. "You've already talked enough to the police, Kelsey," he growled. "They were all over me the day after Shannon died. Now, stay out of this," he warned. "You've done enough."

"You called that morning, didn't you? I remember now. You said something about my secretary being late. What did you want, Douglas?" she demanded. "What did you want from her?"

"What I did or didn't want from Shannon is none of your damn business," he growled dangerously.

"You've already taken everything she had," Kelsey snapped. "What more is there?"

His fingers dug painfully into her arm as he hauled her up close to his sneering face. "Shannon had something that belongs to me and I'm here to take it back.

And if you're really as smart as Shannon always thought you were, you'll stay out of my way." His eyes narrowed into two dark slits.

"Let go of me," she demanded, jerking free of his grasp and reaching for the phone sitting on the dresser. "I suggest you get out of here before the police arrive and throw you out."

"Damn you," he spat out.

But this time Kelsey was prepared, and when he lunged for her, she stepped aside quickly and snatched her purse off the bed and snapped it open. Douglas froze when he saw the small, silver derringer pointed at his heart.

"I said get out," she reminded him, her voice even.

"All right," he said, his face reddening with his rage. "I'm out of here. But you haven't seen the last of me, Kelsey," he warned. "Neither you nor that bitch I was married to have the right to keep what rightfully belongs to me."

"Tell it to your lawyer," Kelsey suggested, her voice hard and her hand steady as she guided him out the door with an impatient wave of the gun.

She watched him lumber down the hall and disappear into the elevator. When she closed the door, she locked it and sagged a moment against the frame, her heart racing and her knees weak.

In a few moments she heard the elevator doors sliding open again and her body tensed. She tightened her grip on her gun and opened the door to peer down the hallway.

Under different circumstances, the sight of Ben holding the doors back with one hand and shoving boxes into the hallway with the other might have been comical, but at the moment all Kelsey felt was relief.

After tucking her gun back into her purse, she walked out into the hallway. "Help is on the way," she promised, hurrying over to relieve him of a stack of six or seven boxes.

"I didn't know how many more we'd need," Ben explained, as he grabbed three more small boxes still inside the elevator. "I may have gone a little overboard."

She smiled at him. "Thanks. I think these ought to just about do it."

When they'd finished hauling the boxes into the apartment, Ben closed the door. Kelsey grabbed two of the smaller boxes and walked into the bedroom.

"Lock it, will you?" she called over her shoulder. "I'm not in the mood for any more surprises."

When he joined her in the bedroom, his expression was sober. "What do you mean 'surprises'?"

"Douglas Hughes. The big guy in the elevator. He must have been getting off just as you were getting on."

"The one who looked like he could play linebacker for the Bears?"

"That's the one," Kelsey confirmed, grimly. "He came by for a not-so-friendly visit. Walked in on me and nearly gave me heart failure."

"What did he want?"

"He said that Shannon had something that belonged to him." His eyes followed hers to the cedar chest. "He wasn't in the mood to explain and he didn't waste any time trying to get what he came for."

"Which was?"

"I don't know. He started rummaging through the cedar chest, but I don't really think he knew for sure that what he wanted was in there," Kelsey said. "Their divorce was settled a few months ago. As far as I know, he has no right to anything in this apartment."

"Why do I get the feeling there's no love lost between the two of you?"

"Because there isn't," Kelsey muttered angrily.

"I say we take a look inside that chest to see if we can figure out what Douglas was so eager to get his hands on."

"My thoughts exactly," Kelsey said. "But I'm telling you right now, even if everything inside that chest has Douglas's name emblazoned in gold, he'll have hell to pay getting his hands on it."

Chapter Six

After Ben made a call to the precinct, he joined Kelsey in the bedroom where they spent the next few minutes examining the contents of the cedar chest. Other than sweaters, blankets and an assortment of mementos and photo albums, the trunk held nothing of real value.

"You can press formal trespassing charges against Douglas Hughes, you know," he reminded her.

She shook her head. "I know and I probably should, but I'm hoping Douglas will come to his senses and back off of his own accord. He has a business to run and he needs to get back to Springfield to run it."

"It's your call," Ben said, satisfied that even though Douglas Hughes was not being charged formally, the call he'd just made would cause Shannon's ex at least a little inconvenience. After all, paperwork did get lost. It happened every day. If a statement was accidentally misplaced or a computer glitch erased an important interview, the police had a duty to take that statement and reschedule that interview, despite any conflicts it might cause the individual citizen.

"Why would Douglas be interested in any of this?" Kelsey said to herself, but loud enough to tug Ben out of his musings. "I'm sure their wedding album means little or nothing to him now. And other than that, I can't see that there is anything in here that even remotely concerns him." Remembering the spiteful way he'd referred to Shannon sent fresh waves of anger rippling through her.

"Do you think we can fit this into the trunk of your car?" she asked.

Ben nodded. "We'll make room for whatever you want to take."

"Thanks," she said, closing the lid. How could she have even considered turning down his offer of help? Cop or no cop, Ben Tanner was proving himself to be a real friend.

"I want to take this box of pictures and the cedar chest home," she said quietly. "The smaller boxes, the ones we stacked by the door, are things I'll be forwarding to Cecil. The rest—the clothes and the linens—I promised to the women's shelter downtown. They're sending someone to pick it all up tomorrow morning."

A heavy silence stretched a moment between them.

"I'm sorry, Kelsey," he said quietly.

"I know. Thank you, Tanner."

"I wish you could get used to calling me Ben," he said as he picked up one end of the chest and she reached for the other.

A smile was all she could manage for a reply. Unfortunately, over the course of the past couple of days, Kelsey had discovered a good many things about Ben that she could "get used to" much too easily, namely his dark good looks, his sexy smile and those incredibly smoky eyes.

After loading the cedar chest into the trunk and filling the back seat with boxes, Ben and Kelsey went back upstairs to the apartment. Kelsey stood in the bedroom door, took a last, long look around and emitted a soft sigh.

Ben moved up behind her and placed both hands gently on her shoulders. His touch surprised her, but she didn't pull away when he turned her around to face him.

"Let's call it a night," he suggested, his voice determined. "I bet you haven't had a thing to eat all day."

He would have won his bet, Kelsey admitted, for other than the diet soda they'd shared over two hours ago and the cup of coffee she'd had this morning, her stomach was empty. Although she really didn't have an appetite, the thought of something warm in her stomach did sound soothing.

"Maybe some soup," she said.

"I know just the place."

"But what about the rest of this?" There were still half a dozen boxes of fragile items that Kelsey didn't want to place in storage.

"I really hadn't planned on coming back here after tonight," she admitted. "And I think we've loaded your car to capacity."

"Well, we've marked everything, right?"

She nodded.

"Then I'll swing by in the morning and pick up the rest and bring them over to your house."

"Oh, I couldn't let you do that . . ." she began, only to find her protest silenced by the gentle pressure of his finger upon her lips. For a moment, she wondered what it might be like if it were his lips pressed against hers instead.

"It's no trouble," he insisted. "And you did say you'd let me help, remember?"

"Yes, but you've already done so much—"

"No buts. I'm starving and you look exhausted. The place I have in mind serves homemade soup like your mother wishes she could make, and sourdough bread and cinnamon rolls so good they charge just for the smell."

She smiled. His offer was too good to refuse. "All right," she relented. "If you're sure you don't mind coming back here in the morning."

"I'm sure."

Kelsey reached for her purse. "But remember, *you* made some other promises, as well. A bowl of soup won't make me forget any of those questions you promised to answer."

"I never thought for a moment that it would," he said as he took her hand and together they headed for the door. "Do you want to take these with you?" he asked, indicating a vase containing three red roses on the nightstand beside the bed.

Kelsey walked over to the vase and studied the flowers. One of them was in full bloom, but the other two had wilted. "I hadn't noticed these," she said, vaguely aware of something gnawing at the back of her mind but feeling too tired and emotionally drained to identify its source.

A florist's card lay next to the vase and Kelsey picked it up. "Next in line," she read. "What does that mean?"

Ben moved up beside her. "Maybe we should ask the sender."

"I don't think we can," Kelsey said, remembering Shannon's so-called secret admirer. She turned the card over and saw the name and address of the florist stamped on the back—Jan's House of Flowers—but there was no indication of the sender's identity.

"There's no signature," she said, picking up the vase and studying the roses.

"Strange. Only one rose survived," he noted, echoing precisely the thought that was going through Kelsey's mind.

"I think I'd like to take this one with me." She drew the rose out of the water, pulled several tissues from a box on the nightstand and wrapped the stem.

"What's this?" Ben asked, picking up the two small pieces of paper that had been obscured until now beneath the vase. "Ticket stubs to the ballet," he noted, answering his own question.

"The ballet?" Kelsey blurted.

"According to the date on the tickets, these seats were for Thursday night. Did Shannon mention anything about going to the ballet?"

She thought for only a moment before she shook her head. "Shannon mentioned the flowers…but these…" She shook her head again as she accepted the ticket stubs he held out to her.

"None of this makes sense," she insisted. "Number one, I was with Shannon until well after seven on Thursday. These tickets are for eight. And secondly, the ballet?" she said incredulously.

"I take it Shannon didn't enjoy the classics."

She shook her head. "The only kind of dancing Shannon would have been interested in was the Texas Two-Step. She was a country music fan, Ben. I doubt if Shannon had ever even seen a real ballet."

"Well, she saved these ticket stubs for some reason. It looks as though the roses and the tickets could have come together."

"It does look that way, doesn't it?"

"Are you sure Shannon didn't mention anything to you about a new man in her life?"

"I'm positive," Kelsey replied quickly. "If the sender of these roses had revealed his identity and gone so far as to ask her to the ballet, believe me, I would have known all the details."

"Let's take these with us," Ben suggested, indicating the florist's card and the ticket stubs. "Someone bought these flowers, and the ballet tickets, as well."

"And maybe that someone was with Shannon after she left me on Thursday night."

"Maybe," Ben said, his tone noncommittal.

And maybe, aside from the stranger in the alley, that someone had been the last person to see Shannon alive, Kelsey speculated as she and Ben walked out of the apartment, and she locked it for the last time.

Clutching the single rose, Kelsey stepped into the elevator. Ben punched the button for the ground floor, and the thoughts that haunted Kelsey's mind landed in the pit of her stomach with a lurch. If someone had been with Shannon on Thursday, had that someone been Shannon's secret admirer or her murderer? Or both?

As BEN DROVE to the restaurant and Kelsey sat beside him, studying the single red rose, she had no way of knowing that hundreds of miles away another young woman, Jennifer White, had received an anonymous red rose, as well.

Like the one from Shannon's apartment, the rose that Jennifer had received was a long-stemmed American beauty. And within its velvety petals lay a secret that bound the three women together in a way that none of them could have ever imagined, not even in their wildest dreams.

At twenty-eight, Jennifer White was the youngest attorney ever hired at the law firm of Grimes, Coble, Armstrong and Eastham. She loved her new job and prided herself on being one of only two female attorneys to work for the firm.

Since graduating from law school and passing the bar, Jennifer had put her personal life on hold. All of her energies were focused on her career. She worked hard, often becoming so immersed in the mound of research the senior partners delegated to her that she lost track of time. Tonight was one such instance.

By the time Jennifer was ready to call it a night, she realized that, except for the janitorial service that made nightly rounds through the fifteen-story building, she was alone. It was a little past ten. If she hurried, she might make it home in time to catch the end of Letterman.

As she gathered her belongings and prepared to leave her small office, her attention was held for a moment by the four long-stemmed roses in the vase that sat on the corner of her desk. Jennifer smiled.

She'd been baffled when a little over two weeks ago the first and second roses had arrived without a card. With the arrival of the third rose a few days later, Jennifer had started to seriously speculate on the identity of her secret admirer.

But until she'd read the card that had accompanied the fourth rose delivered just this morning, she'd been stumped. "To Jennifer. Next in line," the note read. And it had been that cryptic message that had finally given him away.

Jennifer smiled again when she reread the message before tucking the small, white florist's card safely into her purse. "Thank you, Harold," she whispered.

Harold Lathrop had been hired by the law partners just a few days after Jennifer. In a group, he came off as bright and witty. But whenever he and Jennifer were alone, as they had been quite often in the past few weeks preparing for an upcoming trial, Harold seemed shy and self-conscious.

She should have guessed with the first rose, she told herself now, remembering the little ways that Harold had been trying to communicate his feelings. She recalled that morning a few weeks ago when Harold relinquished the copier with his own work only partially completed so that Jennifer could run a report he knew Mr. Eastham had been thundering for.

Then there was the time at the coffee machine when he'd insisted on starting a fresh pot rather than letting her drink the gritty dregs. And just last week when they'd bumped into each other at the grocery store, Harold had stepped aside and let her take his space in line.

"Next in line"—how clever. How romantic! She glanced at the roses again, thinking she really ought to take a moment to toss out the three wilted ones and freshen the water for the one she'd received today. She thought again about the long drive home. Tomorrow would be soon enough, she assured herself. She'd tend to her flowers tomorrow.

At the elevator, Jennifer groaned when she saw the Out of Order sign. Oh, well, she rationalized as she headed for the stairwell, after she'd been stuck behind a desk all day the exercise would probably do her good. Besides, with someone as cute as Harold Lathrop sending her roses, perhaps she ought to start paying more attention to her figure.

At the door with the lighted Exit sign above it, Jennifer became vaguely aware of the sound of a janitor's cart nearby. She opened the door without bothering to look around. She didn't sense the presence behind her, nor did she have time to react when an arm shot out and clamped around her throat, dragging her backward.

The scream that should have echoed through the stark, concrete stairwell was reduced to a muffled whimper when a smothering substance was pressed over her mouth.

With arms flailing and legs kicking, Jennifer fought for her life against the unknown evil that threatened to overwhelm her. Her eyes bulged with terror as she was pressed harder against the steel railing and she was forced to stare down fifteen flights to the ground floor. The pressure on her ribs was excruciating, forcing breath out of her nose in ragged gasps. A startling blow to the back of her head drove her precariously close to unconsciousness, but still she managed to hold on to the railing.

With a surge of strength born out terror, and that most primitive instinct to survive, Jennifer broke free of the iron grasp that held her and whirled around to face her attacker.

An evil smile and a pair of vaguely familiar eyes were the last sights Jennifer White ever saw. The hands that shoved her backward over the railing were steady. The eyes that watched her fall through the stairwell were deadly cold and dispassionate.

When it was over, Jennifer White's murderer opened the door and shoved the janitor's cart back into the hallway before jogging down the stairs to the ground floor. Kneeling over Jennifer's body, he felt renewed, exhilarated and powerful. This had been the easiest yet. Everything was still right on schedule. There had been no passersby this time, no nosey kids at the end of the alley, no suspicious neighbors or prying eyes. The nights he'd spent tracking Jennifer, observing her habits, had paid off in a big dividend.

He whisked the adhesive from Jennifer's flaccid lips with a graceful flick of his wrist. In less than a minute he was out of the building and safely in his car, driving back to Chicago.

The photograph of the pretty blond woman he'd taped to the dashboard captured his attention. The research he'd done on Jennifer White seemed like child's play compared to the intensive study he'd made of Kelsey St. James. It seemed fitting that he had taken the most care, planned in much greater detail for Kelsey's demise. After all, he reminded himself, she would be his last.

THE SMALL CAFÉ on the north side of Lakeview more than lived up to Ben's recommendation. Over a late dinner of homemade vegetable soup and hard rolls, their conversation had run the gamut from the grim details of Shannon's death to happier anecdotes from Ben's childhood in Chicago. And by the time he pulled his car up in front of Kelsey's house, it was after eleven, yet strangely Kelsey felt more rested and more relaxed than she had in several days.

"Thanks for dinner," she said, her hand on the door. "I think a little down time was exactly what I needed."

"Me too," he said. In the glow of the dome light, Kelsey noticed that the tiny laugh lines that winged out from the corners of his eyes seemed a bit deeper. "I'd invite you in for coffee, but I'm afraid I've already monopolized enough of your evening."

"And I'd accept," he said easily, "if I didn't know how tired you must be feeling. I have a lot of ground to cover in the morning, and I suspect you do too."

She was a bit surprised and more than a little disappointed that he'd refused her offer to extend their time together. Throughout the evening, she thought she'd sensed a mutual awareness growing between them. It stung to have him remind her that their time together had a definite purpose. His earlier attentiveness was to be expected, under the circumstances, she reminded herself. What kind of a fool was she to have taken his acts of kindness personally? Undoubtedly the stress of the past few days had affected her normally accurate perceptions, she told herself.

"Yes, it has been a long day," she said. "Should we unload the back seat or the trunk first?"

"Let's take the cedar chest in first," he suggested. In less than fifteen minutes they'd unloaded the trunk and carried the boxes stacked in the back seat into the living room.

"Well, I guess that does it," he said, edging his way past the boxes toward the front door.

"If I come across anything that I think might help in the investigation, I'll call," she said, following him to the door at a safe, impersonal distance. If he could maintain his professional stance, so could she, Kelsey resolved.

"I hope you're not planning on sorting through any of this tonight," he said, turning to her at the door.

Kelsey shook her head wearily as together they stared at the pile of boxes that crowded her small living room. "After that glass of wine with dinner, all I can think about is a warm shower and bed."

The wry smile that crept across his face told her exactly what mental picture her words had drawn. If there had been a way to snatch her words out of the air before they landed on his ears, she would have done it.

"That is without a doubt the best offer I've had all day," he said, his voice low and seductive.

Despite herself, she smiled. "Except that I didn't actually offer anything, now did I, Detective?" Perhaps her intuitive powers weren't so far out of whack, after all.

Ben shook his head, a devilish light dancing in his eyes as he reached for her hand and squeezed it lightly. "No, but a man can dream, can't he?"

She reached past him and pushed the screen door open. "Good night, Detective Tanner," she said in a voice not nearly as firm as she'd have liked.

"Can I at least get a rain check?" he asked. "For the coffee, I mean."

"Of course," she replied, chuckling. "And I never thought you meant anything else but coffee."

"I'll come by in the morning with the rest of the things from the apartment."

"The coffee will be hot and strong."

"Just the way I like it," he said. As he hesitated a moment on the front step, she knew that he was no more ready to bring their evening to a close than she was.

"I'll see you in the morning, then."

She nodded. "I'll be here."

"Good night, Kelsey," he said, backing up a step before finally turning to walk away.

"Ben," she called after him.

He stopped and turned around quickly to face her.

"I just wanted to say... well, I really don't know what I would have done tonight had you not been there. Thanks."

He walked back to where she was standing in the doorway. In the diffused light his eyes were a soft silver-gray. Kelsey's pulse quickened. "You're welcome, Kelsey," he said as he smoothed a strand of hair that had fallen across her forehead. "We're working together, remember?"

For one crazy moment she had an almost irresistible urge to trace each jagged plane of his face with her fingertips. His eyes held hers and her breath caught in her throat when he moved closer and she realized he meant to kiss her.

When his fingers closed gently around the nape of her neck and slowly urged her face toward his, her eyelids fluttered closed. The touch of his lips seemed to breathe life into her body, and she leaned into his kiss. His lips were warm and firm, yet his kiss was achingly tender.

His arms closed around her, and she slid her hands up over his chest and around the back of his neck, suppressing a sudden cry of delight when his kiss deepened.

When he finally dragged his lips from hers, she was breathless. Heat surged through every limb of her body, leaving her weak-kneed and speechless.

"Good night, Kelsey," he said, his voice husky. "Sleep tight. I'll see you in the morning."

She stepped inside, closed the door and leaned against it for a moment, resisting the urge to run to the window like a teenager just to watch him drive away.

Oh, you've really done it now, haven't you, Kelsey? her common sense scolded her even as her heart raced. *You've gone and fallen off the deep end—and with a cop, no less!*

Well, regardless of how he made a living, Kelsey told herself, she'd just experienced the most incredible kiss of her life and she had to tell somebody.

Without thinking, Kelsey plopped down onto the couch, snuggled up to a pillow and reached for the phone. Shannon would never believe this! The receiver was halfway to her ear when she realized what she was doing. With an anguished cry, she buried her face in the pillow and sobbed herself to sleep.

Chapter Seven

Roger McElroy avoided mornings whenever possible. He loathed that time of day when the sun was too bright and people moved and talked too loudly. He especially hated it when those loud-talking, fast-moving people made demands on him before he'd recovered from the activities of the previous night, or even had the chance to finish his second cup of coffee.

Usually, he unplugged his phone and refused to answer the door until after ten. But last night, he'd been so tired that he'd fallen into bed without undressing. He'd slept soundly. He always did after completing a job. It wasn't until the phone began to ring at eight this morning that he opened his eyes again.

Roger was glad he'd answered the phone. The client he was supposed to meet in an hour was motivated, ready to shell out big bucks. Roger's hands shook as he shrugged out of his rumpled clothes. It had been a long time since McElroy Investigations had shown a profit.

He thought back to the voice on the phone as he showered and dressed. The man had sounded agitated, desperate. It was a good sign. Roger could probably name his price, especially if the client wanted him to bend the law, as Roger suspected he did, judging by the sketchy details he'd been willing to give. He hated to burn a friend, but, hey, life wasn't always fair.

Was it fair that he'd had to scrimp for the past five years to merely eke out an existence while Kelsey St. James, a rookie that he himself had helped into the business, turned everything to gold? No, life wasn't fair, but sometimes things worked out, he told himself. Sometimes a sucker got an even break.

Five minutes later Roger walked out of his apartment and jogged down to the street. Sliding his sunglasses onto his face, he glanced at his reflection in the glass before getting into his car. He smiled at what he saw. A professional, a man who had the right connections and knew how to get things done. With a bit of luck, he'd finally be paid for his expertise. Well paid.

Damn, it was good to be alive. And for once, morning didn't seem half bad.

KELSEY SAT in the middle of the living room floor hunched over the open cedar chest. Ben sat behind her on the couch, nursing his second cup of coffee.

"How well do you know Roger McElroy?" he asked, watching for a reaction to the question he'd purposefully pulled from thin air.

"Roger? I guess I know him pretty well," she admitted without looking up. "Why?"

Ben raised his mug to his lips and took another slow sip before he answered. "Well, let's just say he and I share some past history."

"I gathered that much yesterday," she said lightly as she continued to pull things from the cedar chest and stack them onto the floor next to her. "Care to fill me in?"

"I asked first," he said.

She stopped what she was doing, leaned back on her arms and looked up at him. She wore a pale blue cotton blouse that accentuated the color of her eyes. The faded jean shorts she wore exposed her long, golden legs and Ben found he had to steel himself to keep from staring.

"Roger helped me out when no one else in this town would take me seriously," she said.

"I can't imagine anyone taking you anything but seriously," he said, and found himself rewarded with her modest smile.

"You forget who my father was," she said, focusing her attention for a moment on the large leatherbound book she'd pulled onto her lap.

"I hadn't forgotten, but I would have thought his law-enforcement connections would have made things easier for you."

"Maybe they could have, had my father not been dead set against the idea of the agency from the beginning. I guess he'd just assumed a degree in criminal justice meant another cop in the family."

"But you had another idea."

"I did. And as soon as he realized that, he did an about-face, offering to set me up in what would have ultimately become his agency. Unfortunately, when I explained to him that I needed to try and make it on my own, he told me flat out that, without him, I'd fail."

From that day on, she and her father had gone their separate ways, Kelsey went on to explain in a voice that rang with unresolved resentment. She claimed her father's lack of confidence hadn't really surprised her, but Ben could see by the look on her face that it still hurt like hell.

Too bad the old man wasn't still around, Ben thought. He sounded like a man who needed a good swift kick, and at the moment, watching the pain cloud Kelsey's eyes, Ben would have loved to be the man to give it to him.

"It's strange, but in the end my father's disapproval proved to be a powerful motivator," Kelsey said. "I vowed to make the agency a success, but first I knew I needed the savvy that comes only with on-the-job experience to turn my dream into reality. That's where Roger came in."

Ben felt a tightening in his gut.

"He hired me when no one else would. He taught me a great deal."

It didn't matter that she'd worked for McElroy, Ben tried to tell himself. She hadn't been the one who'd run out on him in that alley. She hadn't pulled the trigger. It wasn't possible for someone as basically decent and loyal as Kelsey St. James was proving herself to be to condone the modus operandi of someone like Roger McElroy, was it?

Besides, he told himself, chances were good that even if she had been working with McElroy during that time, she'd had nothing to do with that particular case.

Despite all his rationales, he had to ask, "When did you work for McElroy?"

"The summer before I graduated," she replied easily. "I worked in the office, mainly. Roger thought I was too young to be involved in any of the actual fieldwork. But I learned a great deal just by studying his case files. Why do you ask?'' She looked up at him, her bright blue-eyed gaze openly questioning.

"It's nothing."

"Oh, it's something, all right," she countered. "I saw it yesterday at the cemetery. Now that I've laid out all my morbid family history for you, Tanner, I think it's only fair that you come clean with me."

Beneath all those deceptively soft and alluringly female aspects he found so difficult to ignore, Kelsey St. James was proving to be one tough lady. How her father could have doubted her abilities or her determination was beyond Ben. It was obvious that once she latched on to something, she couldn't be convinced to let go without a fight.

"McElroy and I worked together a few years ago," he began. "It was a bad deal for everyone concerned, but in the end we caught the bad guy. End of story."

She surprised him when she stood up, moved over to the couch and sat down next to him. Her eyes narrowed accusingly; a wry smile touched her full lips as she draped her arm across the back of the couch, her fingertips coming to rest easily on his shoulder. "Sounds like a pretty short story to me, Detective Tanner. Care to elaborate on a few of the more essential details."

"Like?"

"Like a definition of *bad deal* for starters."

All right, he decided, Kelsey wasn't a child. She hadn't asked for, nor did she appear to need, his protection. If she wanted the facts, he'd give them to her. He kept his eyes trained on her face as he spoke. "A little girl was shot and killed when she accidentally wandered into the middle of a drug deal." When she winced, he felt a tug of guilt, but he charged on. "McElroy claimed to have a contact with someone who could identify the shooter. We set up a meeting. Before I knew what was happening, I took a bullet in the chest. The last thing I remember seeing was McElroy's backside getting smaller on the horizon."

When he saw the color drain from her face, he decided against telling her that McElroy hadn't even bothered to stop and call an ambulance until he was safely out of the neighborhood and behind locked doors.

"Oh, my God," she whispered, her eyes wide and unblinking. "I remember hearing about that. Roger was terrified he'd lose his license, or maybe even end up behind bars. I had no idea you were the policeman who was shot."

Ben nodded, his mouth set in a hard line, his stomach churning. Although his feelings were illogical, it bothered him that she'd been associated with McElroy during that horrible time in his own life. Somehow he felt betrayed.

"I wasn't working for Roger then. In fact, I'd just applied for my license and because I'd listed him as a reference Chicago PD was all over me, questioning me about what I did or didn't know about Roger's background. When they realized I'd been little more than a part-time clerk for his agency, they backed off. But for a time I wondered if my involvement with him would hinder my own licensing. A few days later, Roger called me and asked me to intervene for him with my father."

The idea that McElroy had tried to involve Kelsey in his sordid affair sparked fresh anger inside Ben.

"Of course, I couldn't and *wouldn't* ask my father to do anything of the sort," she went on. "Not that he would have considered for one moment siding with a PI over one of his own," she added.

The silence that fell between them was prickly.

"I've never worked with Roger again," she said softly. "Despite all he's done for me, and even though the charges against him were dropped, I found I couldn't work with him after that. I like to think he's still a friend, but professionally... well, we just don't mix."

Ben's relief was nearly palpable.

"I'm sorry," Kelsey said. "Episodes like that give the rest of us a bad name. I hope it hasn't soured you on the entire profession, although I guess I couldn't really blame you if it has."

"I haven't worked with a private investigator since," he admitted. Even within the department, with the exception of Gil Montoya, Ben found he usually worked better alone.

"But you're working with a PI now, aren't you?" she teased.

"Yeah, I guess I am." Impulsively, he reached for her hand. When she returned his playful squeeze, his pulse quickened.

Staring into those soft blue eyes, those eyes that could so easily make him forget all the lessons he'd paid so dearly to learn, he asked, "And how about you, Kelsey? From what you've just told me, you've got a reason or two to be soured against Chicago PD. How do you like working with a cop?"

She looked him squarely in the eye. "You're not like the others." Her quick reply surprised him; he'd expected a curt comeback.

"And is that good or bad?" he asked.

Her slow smile was incredibly seductive. "So far," she said, her husky voice tugging at his heart, "it's been very good. You know, Tanner, for a cop, you're very nearly human." Her teasing tone had returned. "As a matter of fact, I'm beginning to think we might be able to work very well together, don't you?"

He nodded, inhaling the fresh-scrubbed, slightly floral scent of her. For him, being around Kelsey St. James felt like anything but work. Her smile warmed him. Her sense of humor surprised and delighted him. Everything about her excited him.

"And speaking of work..." she murmured. Her expression grew somber as she slid her hand out of his grasp, her gaze wandering to the single red rose in the bud vase on the end table beside them. "What's next?"

"The florist," he said. His throat felt thick with suppressed emotion. He took a sip of cold coffee. "I sent Gil to the address listed on the back of the card. Hopefully we'll have a list of names by this afternoon."

"But if Shannon's mysterious suitor paid cash," Kelsey said, "there won't be a record of the sale."

"I thought about that, as well. Chances are good the sender had the rose delivered. He wouldn't have taken the risk of delivering them in person if he truly wished to remain anonymous. With luck, we might get at least a description from the delivery person."

She didn't look hopeful. Ben knew what she was feeling. Uncovering the trail of a murderer took time.

And no matter how fast they moved, whoever killed Shannon Hughes already had what seemed at the moment to be an insurmountable head start.

AN HOUR LATER Ben offered to deliver the boxes of Shannon's clothes and linens to the women's shelter since they still hadn't arrived. After he'd gone, Kelsey became so engrossed in sorting through the contents of Shannon's cedar chest that she jumped when the phone rang. She grabbed the receiver on the second ring. Kelsey recognized Nelson's voice immediately.

"It's good of you to call, Nelson," she said, letting her gaze wander to the open window in the living room. A tiny bubble of excitement burst inside her at the sight of Ben's car pulling back into the driveway.

"So what do you think?" Nelson asked.

Suddenly embarrassed, Kelsey stammered out an excuse about a faulty phone connection when she realized she hadn't heard a word Nelson had spoken.

"I said, perhaps you ought to consider hiring a temporary to handle the phones and the secretarial duties at the agency, at least for a few weeks, until you can make a more permanent arrangement."

"Well, yes, I guess so," Kelsey replied uneasily, her mind and her heart now achingly aware of his every word.

"I could call them for you, if you'd like."

"I guess that would be all right. Yes, go ahead. Thanks, Nelson."

"I think this is a wise decision," he replied, sounding both pleased and relieved. "I'll contact the temp service this afternoon. When would you like them to send someone over?"

Kelsey didn't know. She hadn't even had time to think about the possibility of someone taking over the position she'd created for Shannon.

"How about tomorrow morning? She can help you field calls," Nelson suggested. "You know you're liable to be deluged your first day back. I don't want to pressure you, Kelsey, but the VanWaters case won't wait much longer."

Kelsey suppressed a weary sigh. She'd have to return to her day-to-day life sometime, and it might as well be tomorrow. Remembering the jumbled files in her office, she said, "Tell them to plan on eight. I'll be there to help whoever they send over get started." Perhaps she could ask Izzy to teach the new receptionist her filing system, Kelsey thought.

"I'll swing by your office around nine, if you think you'll be ready to go back to work," Nelson said. "In the meantime, if you need anything else..."

Ben tapped on the screen door and Kelsey motioned him in. "I'll let you know," she said into the receiver. "Thanks, Nelson. You've been a big help. It was good of you to think ahead for me." And she meant what she'd said. In the past few days, merely dealing with moment-to-moment decisions sometimes seemed impossible, let alone concentrating on the agency business that awaited her when she reopened tomorrow.

"Sounds as though someone is pulling you back into the grind."

"Nelson Masters," she informed him. "And it's probably a good thing that he is. You know, I don't think I realized what a good friend Nelson was before now."

Ben smiled. "A situation like this tends to bring out the best in people. Find anything of interest in all of that?" Ben indicated the pile of papers and pictures stacked beside the empty cedar chest.

Kelsey shook her head. "Besides personal mementos and keepsakes, only an overstuffed expandable file chock-full of old receipts and checkbook stubs. Care to take a look?" She handed him the file and he began sifting though its contents.

"Kelsey, where do you think Douglas fits into the picture?" he asked without looking up.

She shook her head. "I wish I knew. Douglas is a bully. He's got a nasty temper and he's used to getting his own way."

He stopped what he was doing and looked at her, his expression deadly serious. "But do you think he's capable of murder?"

The temperature in the small, sunny room had to be in the seventies, but Kelsey felt a chill. "I've lost a lot of sleep pondering that question."

"And what did you conclude?"

"I honestly don't know," she said slowly. "I mean, how does anyone know what anyone else is truly capable of until after the fact? If he'd been waiting for her that night, if they quarreled...maybe. I guess anything is possible." Her voice faded. "But I'm pretty sure he was never physically abusive to Shannon, at least I believe she would have told me if he had been, especially after the divorce. But after the way he acted last night, I can't help but think he's trying to hide something." But was it murder? Kelsey just didn't know.

"When we questioned him on Friday, he gave us the name of the woman he took to dinner Thursday night, the restaurant they went to and even a description of their waiter. To me his alibi sounded rehearsed, so I had him checked out. I stopped and called my office on the way back from the shelter. Everything he said checks out so far."

"But you still don't seem convinced. What are you thinking, Ben?" She'd never know how pleased he was that she'd finally decided to call him by his first name.

"Only that we need to watch him closely for the next few days. Bursting in on you last night was a desperate act. He's up to something. I've ordered a complete background check. I should have it in my hands by this afternoon."

"When he started shouting last night, I remembered that he'd called the agency Friday morning asking for Shannon. If he had killed her the night before, why on earth would he have called?"

"He could have been trying to shore up his alibi, laying down a false trail."

Was Douglas Hughes capable of such cold-blooded deception? Kelsey wondered. "But if he did murder Shannon, what was his motive?" Kelsey asked. "As I've told you, their divorce *was* bitter, but it was over months ago. Douglas was awarded the house. She gave up her share of their business, he kept his sports car and most of their furniture." In the end, Kelsey guessed Shannon had finally grown tired of fighting him. "All she wanted was out. Damn it …what else does he want from her?" Her voice rose with anger.

Ben's hand came to rest gently on her shoulder. "Whatever it is, I'd say he valued it highly. He took quite a risk confronting you yesterday."

Kelsey hadn't forgotten the warning Douglas had issued. "All we have to do is try to figure out what that something is before he comes after it again," Kelsey said almost to herself as she opened the leather-bound book that lay beside her.

"What's that?" he asked.

Kelsey smiled. "Oh, it's just our senior yearbook. The mighty Rangers of Central High, 1983," she said with forced lightness. He sat down beside her on the floor as she leafed through the pages and stopped her when she reached a page where her picture dominated.

When he whistled appreciatively, she jabbed him playfully in the ribs.

"Homecoming queen, huh? I should have guessed." She groaned and he smiled.

"Is that your mom?" he asked, indicating the smiling woman who was pictured handing Kelsey a bouquet of roses.

"Right again."

"She's a very beautiful woman." His eyes moved from the page to Kelsey's face. "The resemblance is striking."

"Thanks," Kelsey muttered. The blush his compliment caused surprised her. Even more surprising was the way his comment had pleased her.

Ben continued to study the picture. Kelsey knew who he was looking for. "He isn't there," she said. "My father and mother separated when I was five. He moved to Chicago full-time to pursue his career, and we stayed in Willowbend. They made it official when I was fourteen.''

Her parents' divorce was still a bitter chapter in her family's history, and why she'd chosen to divulge a glimpse of that history to Ben now, Kelsey had no idea. But the fact that she had made her feel suddenly vulnerable. An awareness of their shoulders touching made her feel even more exposed. The memory of last night, of his kiss, felt like a tangible presence between them. The emotions Ben Tanner stirred inside her were unlike anything she'd ever felt for a man before. How had it happened so quickly, she asked herself.

"Does your mother still live in Illinois?" he asked, tugging her out of her dangerous daydreams.

"No," she answered quickly, glad to have the chance to focus her attentions on something besides the alarming attraction that seemed to increase by the hour. "Mom remarried shortly after she and my father divorced. She moved to western Montana after I graduated from high school. For the past few years she's been happily nurturing her husband's twenty-acre cherry orchard and his six grandchildren."

"But you chose to stay in Chicago."

"I guess I inherited my father's love of the city," she said, trying without much success to soften the sharp edge of her admission. "Dad offered to let me stay with him until I finished my college degree."

"After all that time apart you must have enjoyed being able to finally spend time with your father."

"Not really," she admitted honestly. Looking back she remembered only the loneliness. "He was always working." To Police Chief Jake St. James, duty came first. "A few months after I moved to Chicago, Shannon became engaged to Douglas. I didn't see her very often after Douglas came into her life and I really missed her. We'd been like sisters growing up, and it seemed Douglas resented our friendship from the beginning."

"So it was just you and your father, at last."

"Just the two of us," Kelsey said. Father and daughter couldn't have been more different if they'd been complete strangers, which in a way she guessed they were. "My last two years of school, I doubled up on courses so that I wouldn't inconvenience him any longer than necessary. I guess we both could have tried harder," Kelsey said with a sigh. "But I'm afraid by then it was too late."

She closed the yearbook abruptly and shoved it off her lap. "I think I'm ready to give this up," she announced. "I don't know what good any of this looking back is doing. We've wasted an entire morning."

Ben disagreed. "I'd hardly call it a waste. The closer we examine Shannon's life—all of it, including the large part she spent with you—the more likely we are to stumble across something that could give us a clue as to what ended it."

She knew he was right. Almost without exception, every investigation she'd ever undertaken had involved digging into the client's past. The hard part was separating her own from Shannon's and somehow remaining objective enough to find a murderer. It was a tall order, one Kelsey didn't know if she felt up to filling.

"I think we've uncovered something through all of this," he said.

"Go on," Kelsey prodded.

"If there ever had been something of value that belonged to Douglas in this chest, I think we can safely assume it isn't there now."

Kelsey shook her head. "I can't figure out why he was so interested in searching through this chest."

"It's hard to second-guess his reasons, but maybe he didn't know where to begin, either."

Ben stood up and walked into the kitchen and brought back the coffeepot. As he refilled both their cups, she focused her attention on a shoe box full of pictures.

"Oh, my gosh!" Kelsey exclaimed, picking out one glossy print. "I can't believe she kept this."

Ben smiled as he stared down at the picture of half a dozen school-age girls dressed in black-and-white leotards posed on a small stage. "Quite a group."

"I really don't believe this," Kelsey said again, laughing. "This must be the only existing record of our very short-lived dance career."

"What were you dressed up for?"

"A recital," she explained. "We were supposed to be dominoes, see? Each of us has a different number of white dots on our costumes."

"Bet I can guess which one you are," Ben said. "You're this one, right? Number one," he declared confidently, pointing to the pretty little girl in the center of the picture whose long blond hair hung in soft ringlets over each shoulder. In her arms she cradled a large bouquet of long-stemmed roses.

"Guess again, Detective," she said teasingly. "I'm the one on the end. The one with the chubby legs. See?"

His expression grew dubious.

"It's true." She laughed. "And see this little girl, the brunette with the freckled nose? Number three. That's Shannon. Wasn't she cute? Back then she was the scrawny one." Suddenly her laughter died.

Without warning, he put his arm around her shoulders and hugged her to him. She nestled into his warmth, swallowing a sob, trying her hardest to dispel the lump in her throat. Blinking back her tears, she stared at the childish faces smiling back at her. Shannon's grin was especially endearing.

Poor little girl, Kelsey thought. How could she have ever known things would turn out this way?

The sound of the doorbell snatched Kelsey back to the present. With a quick swipe at her eyes with the back of her hand, she stood up and hurried to the door.

Ben picked up the expandable file again and began sorting. The odds and ends were the unremarkable remnants of everyday life: utility bills, grocery receipts, coupons, a couple of personal letters and an overdue phone bill. Perhaps the check stubs would prove more meaningful.

He'd picked up the first of a half a dozen and had begun going his way through Shannon's scrawled records when he heard Kelsey walk back into the room. "Who was it?" he called out without looking up.

When she didn't answer, he turned around to face her and felt the shock he saw registered on her face.

"There's no card," she choked out, her voice a ragged whisper. For a moment Ben could only stare at the long-stemmed American beauty rose she held in her hand.

"What the hell . . . ?"

"It's a message," she whispered. "A message from Shannon's murderer!"

Chapter Eight

Kelsey watched in numbed disbelief as Ben charged past her out the front door and chased the florist's van to the end of the block.

A few minutes later, she caught up with him as he was heading back to the house. Unfortunately, his efforts had been in vain. The driver of the delivery van received his orders from all three locations of Jan's House of Flowers. He hadn't even been able to tell Ben which store Kelsey's rose had been ordered from. He worked solely with the florists, he explained to Ben, rarely, if ever, seeing a customer face-to-face.

When they got back to the house, Kelsey looked up the address, and five minutes later they were driving to the closest of the Jan's House of Flowers outlets.

Once inside the store, Kelsey and Ben questioned two of the clerks responsible for both telephone and walk-in orders. Luck was with them, Kelsey decided when they learned that the rose had indeed been ordered from this location.

Unfortunately, neither clerk had taken the order. The initial *A* at the bottom of the ticket belonged to a clerk who was out of the store on her lunch break.

Kelsey and Ben were making plans to come back later, when the clerk, a diminutive young woman with a generous head of curly red hair, walked into the store. The name tag pinned to her pink smock read Amber.

"Yeah," the young woman said, nodding her head vigorously. "I remember that order. Lots of guys come in and buy a single rose," she confided, "but they usually take it with them, you know? They hardly ever want it delivered."

"Why not?" Kelsey asked.

"It's this way," Amber explained. "If a guy is gonna spend the money for a rose, he wants to deliver it in person—you know, more romantic. So he gives his girlfriend the rose with a box of chocolates or something, like for an anniversary or something."

"Do you remember what the man who ordered the single rose looked like?" Ben asked.

The teenager nodded.

"Do you think you could describe him?" Ben asked. Kelsey sensed his impatience.

Amber's freckled face twisted into a frown. "He was, uh, well sort of... businesslike."

"Take your time," Kelsey urged. "In what way was he businesslike, Amber?"

The girl's frown deepened. "Well, he was wearing good clothes. A suit. Blue, I think. Or maybe it was black."

"Was he young or old?" Kelsey asked.

"Oh, he was old."

"How old?" Ben prodded.

"Well, he wasn't as old as you," she blurted out, "but he was pretty old." Amber's face flashed crimson. "Oh, hey, I didn't mean it like that! Oh, man, I'm so embarrassed. You know what I mean, though, right?"

"Right," Ben assured her. Kelsey gave him a sympathetic smile before turning her attention back to questioning Amber. "Do you remember how tall he was?"

Amber seemed uncertain.

Kelsey attempted to make it easier. "Could you look him in the eye or did you have to look up?"

The young woman shifted nervously from one foot to the other; her hands were clenched in front of her and she wrung them furiously. Kelsey reached over and patted the girl's arm reassuringly. "It's okay, Amber," she said. "Just tell us anything you remember. Anything at all."

"I—I'm not sure, but I think he was pretty tall. But to me," she confided, "most everyone seems tall. I guess he was about medium height, for a man. I had to look up."

Perhaps that would rule out Douglas, Kelsey thought. His imposing frame would be memorable, even to the most unobservant witness. "Was he around six feet, do you think or taller?"

"Yeah, six feet. That's right. Well, maybe taller. How tall is six feet, anyway?"

Ben cleared his throat and with her eyes Kelsey asked him to be patient.

They continued to question Amber for another few minutes, and by the time they thanked the young woman and left, Kelsey felt as though she'd been engaged in a wrestling match.

"You were really great with her," Ben noted as they walked back to his car. "No wonder your agency does well."

Kelsey offered him a smile. "Thanks, but I don't feel like we came away with much."

"What do you mean?" he asked, opening the car door and ushering her inside. "We know that he was of medium height or maybe taller. He had darkish brown hair, kind of black. His eyes could have been brown or maybe green, it was hard to tell behind the sunglasses. His clothes were nice—clean and everything! He paid cash and didn't leave his name."

Kelsey groaned. "So what's the problem, Detective? For an ace investigator like yourself, finding him should be a piece of cake, right? All you have to do is arrest half the men in Chicago and hold them until you find the one with a receipt for a single red rose from Jan's House of Flowers in his pocket."

Ben's laugh was dry as he pulled out into the street and guided the car toward Kelsey's office.

"I wasn't trying to be funny," she muttered.

"I know, but look on the bright side. We may have uncovered more information than you think."

"Like what?"

"Well, at least we know which florist the rose came from. And we know it was a man who ordered it."

Kelsey released a small sigh. "It isn't very much, is it?"

"But it's something," he assured her. "You know as well as I do that each piece of the puzzle, no matter how small, eventually helps to reveal the whole picture."

"Like the rose," she murmured, her thoughts drifting back to the solitary rose that had turned their morning upside down. "It was meant as a warning, wasn't it, Ben?" she whispered. "A warning from a murderer."

Ben pulled the car over to the curb in front of St. James Investigations and shut off the engine. With a touch as gentle as a sigh, he kissed her. "We'll find him, Kelsey," he promised. "I won't rest until we do." He kissed her again, and she felt him edging deeper into her heart. She'd been in tight spots before, but never anything as dangerous and frightening as this. But this time was different. This time she wasn't alone.

ONCE INSIDE THE AGENCY, Ben made a call to his office, and Kelsey sank down into her chair and swiveled it around to face the file cabinet. She really ought to start reorganizing. In the process of restoring order to the files, she might even stumble across a clue as to the burglar's motive—funny, the simple break-in didn't seem so simple now.

For the first time in her life, Kelsey felt nearly overwhelmed, physically and emotionally pushed to her limits. It seemed she hadn't had a clear thought since the morning Ben Tanner had walked into the agency and told her Shannon was dead. Ever since that moment her mind had grappled day and night to no avail with the tangle of events that had twisted and turned her life into impossible knots.

Shannon's awful death. The burglary of her office. Douglas Hughes's strange behavior. The roses from the so-called secret admirer. Nothing fit. Nothing made sense. The knot pulled tighter.

The only shred of sanity in the whole jumble was the man standing across the desk from her now, his generous lips set in a firm line as he spoke in low, even tones into the telephone.

He was the kind of man Kelsey wished she'd met under different circumstances, she admitted to herself. She'd never thought she could feel this way about a cop—and he was all cop, a second-generation Chicago cop, at that. He walked like a cop, even talked like one when he forgot himself. There was just no getting around it—he was a cop all the way through to his big heart.

But earlier today she'd told him he was different and she'd never meant anything more. Her invariable mental comparison between Ben and her father had revealed those differences with startling clarity. Jake St. James had been harsh, judgmental and controlling. His criticism and his indifference stung equally. His career had come first and foremost, at the expense of everything and everyone in his life. Weaknesses, real or perceived, were not tolerated. And in others, strengths were hard for him to find. Life was lived by the book, and the book was never wrong. Right and wrong were clearly defined. For Jake St. James there were no rainbows, only black and white.

If it were really true that everyone had an opposite, her father's would have been Ben Tanner—or so it had begun to seem to Kelsey. Like her father, Ben was every inch a professional. But he refused to let a set of arbitrary rules dictate his actions. He was reasonable, funny and kind. He'd set aside his preconceived notions and given her a chance. And so far he'd shown that he valued her opinion and expertise as an investigator. He respected her methods, complimented her way of doing things. He was tough but gentle, warm and affectionate. To Ben, the varying shades of gray in the world were infinite in number.

She glanced at him now, and although he still seemed engrossed in his telephone conversation, his eyes caught hers and held them, communicating an unspoken connection between them. Kelsey felt her heart swell. More than anything in the world she longed to touch him. His eyes told her he felt the same way.

"Thanks, Gil," he said into the receiver. "We'll see you in a few minutes."

"Come on," he said, reaching for her hand as he hung up the phone.

"Where are we going?" she asked as she locked the agency and headed for the car again.

"To my office," he replied, his voice and his expression grave. "I think we just got lucky."

A HALF HOUR LATER, Ben introduced Kelsey to Gil Montoya and the tall dark-haired officer smiled at her as he handed a sheet of curled fax paper to Ben. "Nice to finally meet you, Ms. St. James," he said. "Ben, this fax came in about an hour ago from the FBI in response to your request."

"The FBI?" Kelsey blurted out. When had Ben made that contact?

As though he'd read her thoughts, Ben explained, "I made a call to Virginia last night. Things just seemed a bit too neat, too methodical. I followed a hunch."

Kelsey grasped his meaning instantly, and a shiver zipped down her spine. "You think Shannon's death was the work of a serial killer?"

"I thought it was a possibility worth checking into. The apartment was so clean—not a single print. If not for the bruises and the remnants of adhesive around her mouth, we might have believed it was a suicide or an accident. It could have even been a professional hit, and given Cecil's financial predicament, I still don't think we can ignore that possibility, but then there are those roses, the secret admirer bit—"

"The mob doesn't court its victims," Gil said, shaking his head. "It's a stalker, a very smart, very sophisticated one. I'd bet my next paycheck."

As an investigator, Kelsey found herself fascinated, but as a woman, as Shannon's friend, she was repelled to the depths of her soul. "What does the fax say, Ben?" she asked, forcing a steadiness into her voice that belied her inner trembling.

"According to the FBI there was a similar murder in South Carolina just four weeks ago. A young woman, twenty-seven, found at the bottom of a ravine along a jogging trail. Bruises indicated a struggle. The composition of the remnants of the adhesive found around her mouth match our lab's findings exactly."

Kelsey felt her stomach start to churn. She watched Ben's eyes skim the rest of the page, but he didn't say anything. "What is it, Ben?"

He handed the fax back to Gil. "Roses," he said, his expression dark. "They found long-stemmed roses in her apartment."

She wrapped her arms around herself to still the violent shudder that shook her when the grim truth dawned. "How many?" she asked, her voice ragged. "How many roses did they find?"

Ben shook his head. "They didn't say."

"Can you call them? Can you find out?" She couldn't control the quaver in her voice.

"Certainly," Gil answered. "I'll make the call now."

When the door closed behind Gil, Ben turned to Kelsey. His eyes asked his question.

"Don't you see?" she cried. "If we know how many roses, we'll know how much time I have left."

He was beside her in the space of a heartbeat. "Stop it, Kelsey," he ordered gently. "You've got all the time in the world. I swear I won't let anything happen to you."

When Gil walked back into the office a few minutes later, Ben's arms were still wrapped around Kelsey. Self-consciously, she moved quickly out of his embrace.

If Gil realized he'd intruded on their intimacy, his expression didn't reflect it. What it did reflect was bad news, Kelsey knew instinctively.

"Two roses," he said flatly. "They found them with an unsigned card in her bedroom."

"Shannon was three," Kelsey whispered.

Ben's expression grew stony. "It may look like a pattern, but we're not ready to jump to any hard and fast conclusions yet."

"That means I must be number four," she said as though she hadn't heard him. The haunted look in her eyes caused Ben's stomach to lurch as though he'd just stepped into an open elevator shaft.

"No, Ms. St. James," Gil said, his voice dropping a notch. "The FBI just got a report that says the St. Louis police found number four last night."

WAITING FOR THE REPORT to come in from St. Louis was maddening. As Kelsey reread the fax from the FBI, Ben handed her a yellow pad and instructed her to draw two vertical lines down the center.

"At the top of the first column write Shannon Hughes," he said. "At the top of the second, write Theresa Youngblood." Before Kelsey could ask, he added, "That was the name of the victim in South Carolina." He set a can of diet soda down in front of her, and she nodded her thanks.

"We need to compare everything we know about these two women," Ben said.

When Kelsey explained that her experience in investigation had never included anything as detailed as tracking a serial killer, Ben understood her frustration. "I don't pretend to be an expert in that area either. But right now it's not his methods that pose the mystery."

The method, as Ben had referred to it, employed in both crimes was horrifyingly similar. The fall made to look like an accident or suicide, the bruises on the victim's body, the telltale remnants around the victim's mouths where some sort of adhesive had been used to stifle their screams. And of course, the roses.

Kelsey wondered if ballet tickets had been recovered in South Carolina. When she asked, Ben nodded, his expression grim. Would there be a set of ballet tickets waiting for her when she got home, Kelsey wondered morbidly.

And as if he'd read her thoughts, Ben added, "We need to focus our attention on the victims, Kelsey. We'll be looking for any commonality between Shannon and Theresa. We'll factor in the third victim as soon as the details come in from St. Louis." Kelsey saw that his handsome face was drawn.

"If we're lucky, we'll discover a single thread running through each of their lives," he added.

"And if that thread is strong enough," Kelsey said, looking up into his eyes, "we just might reel in a killer."

"Exactly," he said as he put his arm around her shoulders and gave her a reassuring hug.

"I wish I knew what I was looking for," Kelsey said.

Ben pulled a chair up beside her and sat down. "We're looking for everything and anything—physical characteristics, life-styles, backgrounds. He might have chosen his victims based on something as simple as hair color or as obscure as the type of car they drove."

"It sounds like a rather haphazard, hit-or-miss investigative technique," Kelsey said.

"It does seem that way," Ben admitted. "But it's a proven method. The best chance, maybe the only chance, we have to stop this guy, to short-circuit his pattern is by knowing what that pattern is and being prepared for his next strike."

Kelsey felt goose bumps spring up on her arms. Did the rose delivered this morning mean she was about to be his "next strike"? She shook her grim thoughts away and began recording data on the tablet.

"The FBI is doing exactly what we're doing," Ben informed her. "Feeding information about Theresa and Shannon into their computers even now."

Kelsey put her pen down. "What can I possibly add that the FBI wouldn't already have?"

''You bring the most important kind of information to this case. You were Shannon's best friend. The FBI, Chicago PD and any other law-enforcement agency can only be successful with the help of people like you.''

From her own experience, Kelsey knew what he said was true. An investigation was only as solid as its best witness. But all the same, she couldn't help feeling overwhelmed. Investigator, friend or potential victim? Which role should she assume to try to stop a demented killer?

AN HOUR LATER, Kelsey was still trying to fill the columns on the long, yellow pad. Shannon and Theresa had been within months of being exactly the same age. Both had been divorced. Shannon was a brunette. Theresa Youngblood had been a blonde. Shannon had been a receptionist, Theresa, a hairstylist with her own shop. She had two children.

Kelsey's heart ached for Theresa's family, for the children who were now forced to grow up without their mother.

Kelsey noted that both Shannon and Theresa had been born in Illinois. It wasn't much, but it was something. She swiveled around in her chair to tell Ben, but saw he had left the office and was standing over Gil's desk, absorbed in a conversation that, judging by the fact that they both turned and looked at her at the same time, had everything to do with her.

Kelsey stood up and stretched, reaching around to massage the knotted muscles in her neck and shoulders. She glanced out the window and was startled to see that it was already dark.

Ben and Gil walked into Ben's office together. "Finished with your list?" Ben asked.

She shook her head. "Just taking a breather," she said. "But I did come across something interesting. Take a look," she said, handing him the tablet. "Shannon and Theresa were both Illinois natives."

He nodded, but his expression was noncommittal.

"I know it isn't much," she said. "But at this point I don't think we can ignore anything, or write any similarity off as coincidence."

Kelsey reached to take the tablet back, but instead of handing it to her, Ben gave it to Gil.

"I think we'd better call it a night, Kelsey," Ben said.

"But I'm not finished," she insisted. As difficult as she knew it would be, she planned to create a third column with her own name at the top. She told Ben as much and his expression darkened as though a shadow had moved across his face.

"It's late, Kelsey. Grab your purse. I'm taking you out to dinner and then home."

His not-so-indirect order struck a sour chord deep inside her, reminding her of the way her father had made everything sound like an order. "Gee, how could a girl refuse such a charming offer? Should I fall out or salute?" She saw immediately that her sarcasm had hit its mark. His eyes narrowed and he ran a hand impatiently through his hair.

"We've been at this all day, Kelsey, and we're both tired—" She noted the dark smudges that had begun to darken beneath his eyes, and she was ready to concede to his logic until he added, "Don't you think it's a bit late for a power struggle?"

"What on earth is that pigheaded statement supposed to mean?" she snapped, vaguely aware of Gil slipping out of the office and closing the door behind him.

"Give me a break, Kelsey, all right? I'm not your father. I know when to punch the time clock even if you don't. Now let's drop the defiant teenager routine and get the hell out of here."

No, he wasn't her father. And up until now Kelsey had thought Ben incapable of firing the kind of verbal ammunition that her father had always been so adept at using. But even Jake himself couldn't have chosen the words to pierce her heart and wound her pride any deeper than Ben Tanner had just done, Kelsey realized. A thousand stinging replies choked her, but the bite of hot tears in her eyes rendered her speechless. Brushing past him, she stalked toward the door.

He grabbed her arm, but when she turned and said, "Get your hands off me, Tanner," he released her immediately, as though her skin had singed his fingertips.

With head held high, Kelsey marched past Gil's desk and out the double doors of the homicide office. At the stairway, she took the steps two at a time and emerged breathless on the ground floor. With vision blurred by anger and hurt, she reached the darkened street.

Luck was with her. The first taxi she hailed pulled over to the curb. "Printer's Row," she barked as she slammed the door so hard that the cab shook. "La-Salle Street."

"You got a problem, lady?" the cabbie asked gruffly over his shoulder.

She dismissed his concern with a wave of her hand and a curt shake of her head. She did have a problem, she told herself, and it was a big one. But thanks to the harsh lessons she'd learned early in life—lessons that Ben Tanner had almost persuaded her to forget—she was prepared to face her problems the way she'd always been forced to face them in the past. Alone.

Chapter Nine

An incessant drumming sound tugged Kelsey from a deep, dreamless sleep. With a shake of her head, she tried to make the pesky noisy go away, but the drumming turned to pounding and the noise grew louder.

With a start, she sat up and found she had to catch herself to keep from falling off the small couch in the corner of her office. Her neck felt as if she'd used a rock for a pillow. Her back and leg muscles screamed. And the pounding from the outer office continued.

When she finally staggered out of her office, Kelsey saw Roger McElroy at the outer door. "Just a minute," she called out. "Hang on."

She fumbled for a moment with the lock before she opened the door.

"Hey, kid. What happened to you? You look like hell."

"Thanks, Roger," she muttered over her shoulder as she shuffled back into her office. "What time is it?"

"Almost seven."

Kelsey walked into the small bathroom connected to her office and turned on the water. Bending over the sink, she splashed cold water on her face and pressed a towel over her eyes. "Didn't you used to hate mornings? What are you doing here at this ungodly hour?" she asked as she dried her face and hands and ran a brush through her hair.

Roger seemed not to have heard her question. He was staring at the couch and the rumpled afghan. "You slept here, didn't you, kid? Geez, no wonder I couldn't raise you at home."

"Sleep isn't exactly the word," she muttered. "But I'm awake now, so why don't you tell me what couldn't have waited until business hours." Kelsey plopped down in the chair behind her desk.

Roger settled himself on the couch and blew out a long exasperated breath that smelled of coffee and cigarettes. "Damn, I don't know where to start."

"Just get to it, Roger," Kelsey said impatiently. "I'm not in the mood for games."

"It's the old man. Cecil. Shannon's dad."

Kelsey felt all her senses quicken and she leaned forward in her chair. "What about him, Roger? Is he in some kind of trouble?"

Roger nodded, but seemed reluctant to say more. "You probably knew the old man had been playing with some pretty rough characters."

"So I've heard," she said, and wondered how Roger knew about Cecil's debt to the loan shark.

"I know they're after him," he said as though he'd been privy to her thoughts. "He owes them some big dough and they want it. They want it bad."

"Who?" Kelsey demanded.

Roger stood up and walked over to the window and spoke with his back to her. "I wouldn't tell you if I knew, kid. These guys play hardball. Trust me, you don't want to know their names."

Kelsey bit down on her anger. "Don't patronize me, Roger," she said sharply. "You're here for a reason. Now what is it? What has any of this got to do with me?"

Roger turned around slowly. Kelsey found his flair for the dramatic especially irritating this morning. "The old man told certain parties that he was getting the money he owed them from his daughter."

Kelsey felt her blood turn cold in her veins. "Go on," she urged him, thinking that Ben's theory that Shannon had died at the hands of organized criminals might not have been so far off, after all.

"Don't you get it? It's a hop, skip and a jump from Shannon to you. If she had that money, they figure you've got it now."

Kelsey felt like screaming; it was just too early for Roger's double-talk. "What do you mean, Roger? What has any of this got to do with me? Did Cecil give someone my name? Is that it? Did he tell them I had the money?"

Roger's silence was a grim affirmation of her worst nightmare. Frustration, anger and something close to panic welled inside her. Before she knew what she was doing, she was out of her chair, around the edge of the desk and standing in front of him.

"Damn it, Roger, tell me what you know," she demanded. "I want names. Who are these people and what do you have to do with this?"

He took a defensive step backward. "Hey, back off, Kelsey," he snapped. "I came here to help you out. But I can walk right out and let you sink. It's no skin off my teeth. I'm doing you a favor and I don't need this abuse."

Kelsey glared at him, realizing bitterly that Roger McElroy wouldn't help his own grandmother unless there was a buck in it for him. He'd only cultivated Kelsey's friendship when he'd thought her father could do him some favors within the department. He was a con man who worked both sides of the law. The way he'd left Ben for dead was a chilling reminder of his cowardice.

But regardless of what she thought of Roger, she'd have to get control of her emotions if she hoped to get any information out of him. "I'm sorry," she managed to say. "I've been through a lot lately. It's been a long week."

"Well, that's better," he said, his expression smug as he smoothed imaginary wrinkles from his shirtfront. "I'm gonna help you out, kid, 'cause I like you. I got connections. I think I can fix this up for you. But you've got to do what I tell you, down to the letter. Just remember that, and no one will get hurt, understand?"

Kelsey nodded uneasily. "Tell me what I have to do."

Roger sat back down on the couch and toyed with the creases at his knees. "Before she died, Shannon told her old man she'd raised the money he owed. She said she had it in cash. My client wants his money back."

"Your client!" she exclaimed.

"My client," he reiterated. "He wants his money back. In exchange, he's willing to turn over the guy who killed Shannon."

Kelsey's knees bent involuntarily and she sank down into her chair, her mind whirling. "But... but I don't have that money," she stammered. "I don't know anything about it... what Shannon might have done with it, where it might be hidden." Or even if it ever existed, she thought desperately.

"You packed up all her things, didn't you?" Roger asked, his eyes dull as he leaned forward in his seat. "It's got to be in there somewhere. Twenty thousand bucks. That's a lot of cash. That much dough doesn't just disappear by itself."

"And what if I do find it? Then what?"

"I'll handle everything from there."

"What do you mean?" she asked suspiciously.

"I'll make the delivery, square things with my client. He'll get his money and you'll get the name of your killer." He rose, planted his hands on her desk and leaned closer. "If you don't come up with that cash, I can't help you, kid. As I said, these guys play hardball. I won't be able to save you from them. I can't protect the old man much longer, either. Yeah, they know everything. They've had him located for the past forty-eight hours."

The idea of Cecil's life, her own life and the apprehension of Shannon's murderer resting in the unethical hands of Roger McElroy sent a shiver of dread through her.

"How much time do we have?" Kelsey asked, her voice much steadier than her pulse rate.

"I'll be in touch with you tonight," he said. "Don't make any plans. And stay away from that cop boyfriend of yours. I'll call you at home. Late. After eleven. You'd better be sure you're there."

She glared at him as he turned to leave.

"Don't even think about calling the police in on this, Kelsey," he warned at the door. "My client holds a lot of markers down at City Hall. You know what I mean?"

Kelsey knew all too well. Her own father had made a crusade of rooting out and exposing corrupt city officials and cops on the take. She only wished now that Roger McElroy had been one of the rats caught in her father's trap.

For a moment after he left, Kelsey held her breath, dreading the moment when the next shoe might drop and knowing that when it did, the sound would be deafening.

BY THE TIME Francine, the young woman from the temporary service, showed up, Kelsey had changed into a pale blue silk skirt and blouse and a pair of low-heeled pumps she kept in her office for emergencies.

Izzy showed up a few moments later, explaining that since it was her day off, she had decided to come in and help Kelsey get the agency reopened. On such an unsettling morning, Kelsey appreciated Izzy's kindness more than she could ever express.

For the next hour Izzy and Francine worked on the files in Kelsey's office. Just before nine, Kelsey slipped into the reception area for a much-needed first cup of coffee. Her mind had been working overtime since Roger McElroy's disturbing visit.

If what Roger said was true, he had somehow become privy to information about a dangerous and demented serial killer. To Kelsey it seemed unlikely that

Roger possessed information that had eluded both the Chicago police and the FBI.

But what if the authorities were wrong in their theory of a serial killer? What if Shannon's murder really *had* been connected to her father's involvement with the loan shark, as Ben had first suspected? Within that scenario, Roger McElroy just might be telling the truth. And if he was, by tonight Kelsey might know the identity of Shannon's murderer.

All she had to do was come up with the cash that Shannon had planned to give Cecil, anyway. Twenty thousand dollars. Somehow it seemed a small price to pay to bring Shannon's killer to justice. It was a chance Kelsey was prepared to take, a price she was willing to pay.

When the phone on the front desk rang, Kelsey grabbed it before the second ring. "St. James Investigations," she said.

"Good morning, Kelsey." Her stomach did an elevator drop. Whether she liked it or not, a thousand little things about Ben Tanner had already become a permanent part of her memory, and the sound of his deep, sexy voice was one of them.

"What do you want?" she asked, fighting to keep the emotion out of her voice.

"You," he said simply.

Her heart galloped. "You're crazy."

"And I think you want me too, Kelsey, if you'd just admit it. Or do you still feel like smashing my fat head in?"

Despite herself she smiled. "I didn't say you were a fathead, Tanner," she corrected smugly. "I said you were pigheaded."

"And you were right. Sometimes I am. Now tell me what it'll take to make amends, to make you want to kiss me again?" She could picture his wry smile, almost taste his lips and the anger around her heart melted like a Sno-Kone on a Chicago sidewalk in July.

"I'm available for lunch."

"And I know the perfect place."

"Noon?"

"I'll pick you up," he said. "That is, if it's all right with you?" he added hastily.

"Don't overdo it, Detective," she warned playfully. "You know how we defiant types hate to be patronized." Kelsey found it difficult to maintain her cool demeanor when at the moment being with Ben Tanner again was what she wanted more than anything else in the world.

She was still holding the phone when Nelson Masters walked in the door. "Am I interrupting?" he asked.

"No, of course not," she replied, hastily replacing the receiver. "I was waiting for you, Nelson. Come in. Let's get started. Hopefully we can put together the rest of the VanWaters file this morning."

They could accomplish a great deal before lunch, Kelsey told herself as she and Nelson settled down to work. Three hours wasn't really such a long time. But to Kelsey, waiting to be with Ben again felt like an eternity.

BY ELEVEN-THIRTY they had finished the VanWaters report. Kelsey could hardly believe she'd been able to clear her mind long enough to concentrate on the workers' compensation case, but strangely, immersing herself in the details of the case had proven to be an effective distraction for her swirling thoughts. Out of nowhere, something her father had once said about an hour of honest work beating an hour on a therapist's couch flashed through her mind.

"You did a thorough job of research in investigating this case, Kelsey," Nelson said, beaming. "One of the best things I ever did for Consolidated Universal was to recommend your agency."

"Thank you, Nelson," she said as she stood up and prepared to walk with him to the door.

"How about some lunch?" he asked. "Consolidated's treat."

"Oh, thanks, Nelson, that sounds wonderful, but I'm afraid I've already made plans."

His expression reflected his disappointment. "I knew I should have asked sooner. I was hoping we could spend some time together to talk about...all that's happened."

"I'm sorry," she said, laying a hand gently on his sleeve. "Maybe next time."

He reached for the door to the outer office, but he didn't open it. "Have the police said anything about what they think happened to Shannon?"

Kelsey felt a stab of grief. Though she and Ben had discussed little else over the past few days, she'd come to realize that she'd never get used to her loss, and that discussing Shannon's death would never come easily.

"She was murdered," she said quietly.

His face paled. "Oh, my God," he gasped. "Do they have any idea who...?"

"So far they haven't made any arrests."

Nelson slumped against the door. "Murdered," he whispered. "That's so awful, so unbelievable. When I heard she had fallen, I guess I just assumed it was an accident or—"

Kelsey nodded. "I know. Everyone was shocked."

"I just keep thinking about the last time we spoke," Nelson said. "When she was so eager to cash in that policy, I should have sensed she was in some kind of trouble. If only I could have done something. Maybe—"

"What are you talking about, Nelson?" Kelsey interrupted. "What policy?"

"She didn't tell you? She was so excited by her windfall, I just assumed she'd told everyone."

"Shannon never mentioned anything about a policy to me." And Kelsey couldn't help wondering why she hadn't.

Nelson went on. "Shortly after she moved into her new apartment, she found an old life insurance policy that had been purchased for her by her grandparents as a christening gift. She told me she'd forgotten the policy even existed until she ran across it mixed in with some other papers when she was unpacking."

Kelsey's thoughts leaped immediately to Douglas. Had Shannon told *him* about the policy? Was that what he'd been looking for? But if so, why? If the life insurance policy had been issued when Shannon was an infant, Douglas couldn't have been named the beneficiary.

"Shannon brought the policy to me and asked for my advice," Nelson explained.

Kelsey nodded, telling herself that it was only natural that Shannon had consulted Nelson first about something so obviously within his range of expertise. But why hadn't she come to Kelsey later, she wondered, feeling a nip of something uncomfortably close to jealousy. "What kind of advice, Nelson?" she asked. "Can you tell me?"

"She wanted to know how much the policy was worth and how to go about cashing it in." His expression was disapproving. "Of course I tried to talk her out of it. Before his death, her grandfather set up an ongoing trust to cover the policy, so it wasn't a matter of Shannon not being able to afford the yearly premiums. Anyway, after examining the policy and making a phone call to the insurance company that issued it, I discovered the policy had accumulated an eighteen-thousand-dollar surrender value. Shannon was quite excited."

Kelsey could well imagine that she had been. With Cecil's neck on the line, the money must have seemed like a gift from heaven. Eighteen thousand dollars. That explained why Shannon had asked to borrow two thousand from Kelsey—it was the difference between the cash value in the policy and what Cecil owed the loan shark.

"I tried to explain to Shannon that if she just let the policy keep growing, it would be worth much more to her when she really needed it."

Nelson's advice was exactly what she would have advised, as well, Kelsey told herself. She would have begged Shannon not to turn the money over to Cecil, but to use the sudden windfall for her own fresh start. Perhaps that explained why Shannon had chosen to keep the policy a secret from her best friend.

"And how did Shannon react to your suggestion?" Kelsey asked, although it wasn't too difficult for her to guess what Shannon's response would have been. Cecil's problems notwithstanding, Shannon had always possessed a live-for-today attitude.

"She just laughed," Nelson replied. "She said, 'I don't think I'll ever need it more than I need it now.' I should have known then and there that she was in some kind of trouble," he confided. "I just wish I could have helped her more." His voice faded.

"We thought we *were* helping," Kelsey explained for Nelson's benefit as well as her own. "But in the end, Shannon had to do things her own way."

A wistful expression crept into his eyes. "Though I hadn't known Shannon long, I admired her a great deal."

"I know you did. And she considered you her friend, too," Kelsey assured him softly.

Nelson swallowed hard, and when he started speaking again, his voice was gruff. "Anyway, when I heard that she'd fallen from that balcony... that she was dead—" his eyes fell away from hers and he shook his head "—well, I'm ashamed to tell you what I thought she'd done."

Kelsey clasped her hands in front of her to still their trembling. "It's all right, Nelson," she soothed. "Don't punish yourself. For those first few hours, none of us knew what to think."

For a long moment neither of them said anything.

At last it was Nelson who broke the silence. "Well, I guess I'd better get back to my office."

Kelsey opened the door for him. "Nelson, do you know if Shannon ever cashed that policy?"

He shook his head. "I don't know. We never talked about it again." He cleared his throat. "I'll call you tomorrow, and let you know how the negotiations go with VanWaters."

As the door closed behind him, Kelsey sighed, acknowledging the heaviness that settled over her heart. The effect of Shannon's death was like a pebble tossed into a pool, the effects continuing to ripple in an ever-widening circle.

As Kelsey walked back to her desk, she thought of Vanessa Overholt. Surely if Shannon had needed help in cashing the insurance policy, she would have gone to her lawyer. Kelsey picked up the phone and dialed Vanessa's office. When Vanessa came on the line, Kelsey dived into the subject of the policy immediately.

"I'm as surprised by all of this as you are," Vanessa said after Kelsey had explained. "And frankly, I'm a bit disappointed. I thought Shannon considered me more than just her lawyer."

"I know she did, Vanessa," Kelsey offered.

"Well, this is some way to treat your friends, isn't it? Shannon Hughes died owing me over ten thousand dollars when she had eighteen thousand in cash on hand."

Kelsey felt as though she'd been punched. Ben had been wrong when he'd said the death of a friend brought out the best in people. In Vanessa Overholt, Shannon's death had brought out the worst. "I've got to go, Vanessa," Kelsey said coolly. "If I find the money, I'll see that you get paid."

Vanessa's tone brightened measurably when she said, "I'd appreciate that, Kelsey. Please keep me posted."

"Yeah, sure, Vanessa," Kelsey muttered to herself after she hung up the phone. "You'll get yours when Douglas Hughes gets his."

Kelsey glanced at her watch; realizing it was almost noon jolted her into action. She just had time to put on fresh lipstick and run a brush through her hair before Ben arrived.

Standing in her office doorway, watching him walk in, she couldn't help but notice the admiring looks cast by Izzy and Francine as they greeted him and ushered him into her office.

As soon as she closed the door behind them, he swept her into his arms. "God, you feel good," he breathed against her cheek. His actions startled and pleased her in a way she'd never thought possible. She hugged him back, pressing her body against his muscular frame, reveling in his open display of affection.

"I'll never forget how I felt when you walked out on me," he declared, pulling her gently away from him and holding her at arm's length. "I couldn't stand the thought of never seeing you again, Kelsey. And I'm warning you, next time you won't get away from me without one hell of a fight," he admitted, his voice heavy with emotion. "But I know I hurt you and I'm sorry."

"You made me angry," she corrected.

"I hurt you," he said again. "You trusted me. You confided in me and I threw it back in your face. Forgive me. I promise it'll never happen again."

"But you were right," she said. "It had been a long day. It was time to give it a rest. I was wrong." For some reason it wasn't difficult admitting it to him.

He brought his fingertips to her lips. "I say we compromise. We were both wrong. Stupid. Stubborn and—"

"Pigheaded," they blurted out at the same time.

Her laughter was smothered by his kisses. His mouth bore down on hers with a force that shocked and delighted her at the same time. His hands slid up her back, urging her closer, his seemingly insatiable desire igniting her own passion. She clung to him, relishing the feel of his solid strength. Her fingers pressed harder into the muscles in his back, and a groan of desire escaped his lips as his mouth sought hers again and again.

Kelsey felt her passion melding with his and she longed to go on kissing him forever, but the sound of the telephone ringing in the reception area jerked her back to reality. Breathlessly she withdrew from his embrace.

Try as she might, she couldn't come up with a clever quip to dispel the sexual tension that simmered between them. "I—I don't know what to say," she stammered.

"I think you were about to forgive me," he said in a sexy whisper.

She ran a hand over his tousled hair and smiled. "I guess I was," she admitted. "And you were about to take me to lunch, right?"

They were oblivious to Izzy's knowing smile when they walked out of Kelsey's office. As a matter of fact, other than each other, they hardly saw anything at all.

BEN DROVE to the north-side café where they'd eaten dinner on Monday night. When they arrived, Kelsey was disappointed to see that the restaurant was jammed. She'd already decided to tell Ben everything that had transpired between her and Roger McElroy. But trying to explain her precarious position over the din in the restaurant didn't seem possible. Besides, she couldn't afford to run the risk that their conversation might be overheard.

"We need to swing by my house on the way back to the agency," she said. "I've got something to tell you that can't wait." Relief flooded her when the waiter finally made his way to their table and Ben ordered their food to go.

Forty-five minutes later they were sitting at the redwood picnic table, in the shade of an ancient elm tree in Kelsey's backyard. Ben ate his sandwich without tasting it as he listened to Kelsey explain the details of her morning encounter with Roger McElroy, and her subsequent discussion with Nelson Masters concerning Shannon's insurance policy.

"Roger is supposed to call me tonight to give me instructions." She had related the gist of her conversation with McElroy calmly, but Ben could see the worry in her eyes. "Ben, I don't have any idea where Shannon might have stashed that money, if she ever had it."

"What about the insurance policy?"

"We didn't run across it in any of her papers. She may have cashed it, but I just don't know. There's no way I can raise that kind of cash in less than ten hours. What am I going to do?"

"You're not going to do anything," he said impulsively. When he saw her eyes suddenly narrow, he added, "Without me to back you up, that is."

"Roger warned me against going to the police. He said they know where Cecil is and that they won't hesitate to go after him." He detested the fear that passed like a shadow over her eyes.

"You didn't go to the police," he said flatly, reaching for her hand. "At least not as far as anyone is going to know until it's too late to matter. We're going to give them what they want."

"You can't mean that."

"I do. We're going to give them their money, but just long enough to find out who Roger is working for."

As Ben explained how he intended to set it up, Sherlock sauntered over and laid his head on Kelsey's lap. As she stroked the dog's head idly, Ben could see her mind working. Without her uttering a word, he knew all the obstacles she was imagining. They were the same ones he was mentally checking off in his own mind.

"We don't really have a choice, do we?" she said.

"No. We don't. I don't believe for one second that they intend to turn over Shannon's murderer, if they even know who he is. Once you give that money to Roger McElroy, he'll make his connection, collect his fee and disappear. I'd bet the whole twenty thousand on it."

"You could be right," she said. "I've heard that his agency is in financial trouble," Kelsey added. "More than once he's complained that he's never been paid what he's worth, that his expertise has always been underrated."

"What did he say about Cecil? Do you think he might have been bluffing?"

Kelsey shook her head. "He seemed confident. And even if he was bluffing, I think we've got to assume that he and his client have every advantage."

"You're right. Never underestimate your enemy," Ben agreed, admiring her savvy and wondering how she had obtained that much wisdom with her limited experience.

She picked at her salad indifferently before finally tossing the fork down on the table. "We have no guarantee that Cecil will be safe even after we pay off his debt."

"Or you, either," he reminded her. "These people are greedy. Once you give in to their demands, they come back for more. They're never satisfied. Trust me—the only way to stop them is to put them out of business. Our plan will work." All Kelsey had to do was hand over the money to Roger. He'd gladly take it from there, he told himself.

"But we don't have the money, Ben. How are we going to come up with twenty thousand dollars by tonight?"

He stood up and walked around the table and took her hand and kissed it. "I guess I never told you about my rich uncle, did I?"

"No, I don't think you ever did," she replied suspiciously. "But if he's the generous type, I'd love to meet him now."

"I need to call the precinct," he said and walked into the house. After a quick conversation with Gil, he returned to the porch. "If you're ready to go back to the agency, I'll drive you and then I'll go pick up the money."

Kelsey's expression was incredulous. "Just like that? One phone call to Gil Montoya and the money is as good as ours? What's going on, Tanner? You know if Roger's contact spots phony money or marked bills this whole deal could blow up in our faces."

"The money will be real, all right," he assured her, placing a hand in the middle of her back as he ushered her out of the house.

As they walked toward his car together, Ben thought of how Chief St. James was probably doing a three-sixty in his grave at the way Ben planned to borrow the twenty thousand dollars—money from a recent drug bust—from the precinct's evidence room without authorization.

"I want to know where that money is coming from, Ben," Kelsey said flatly as he opened the car door and she folded into the passenger's seat.

He frowned. "Let's just say it's sort of like a fairy tale," he said before closing the door and walking around to the driver's side.

"But what kind of fairy tale has a twenty-thousand-dollar jackpot?" she demanded as he slid in behind the wheel and started the engine.

"Cinderella," he told her. "But instead of a glass slipper or a silver coach, it's cold hard cash. And if we don't get it back home by midnight, Gil and I will turn into a couple of pumpkins." A couple of suspended pumpkins, with criminal charges hanging over their heads, he added to himself grimly.

But what choice did he have? Going through proper channels, wading through the paperwork and cutting all that official red tape took time, precious time they didn't have and couldn't afford to spend so long as a killer was still stalking Kelsey.

The man who had sent her the anonymous roses was the most dangerous kind of killer, one whose actions were dictated by a bizarre set of rules that originated somewhere in the depths of a demented and tortured mind. Bending the rules, even risking his career, seemed a minor inconvenience to Ben when measured against the chance he might be buying, the chance to stop the animal who wanted to end Kelsey's life.

"Kelsey, I want you to trust me on this," he said gravely. "Believe me, it's better if you don't know any more about where the money is coming from."

He saw her measuring his request. Kelsey was bright, naturally inquisitive, focused and determined—traits that enhanced her irresistibility as far as he was concerned. But she was stubborn, too. She had a personal stake in every aspect of this case, and asking her to back off, even an inch, was asking a great deal, and he knew it.

"Please?" he added, searching her blue eyes for the understanding he had no right to expect.

She gazed back at him. "All right," she said finally. "But when this is all over—"

"I know, I know." He smiled. "You'll have a lot of questions."

She leaned over and gave him a quick kiss on the cheek. "And you'll have all the answers, right, Detective?"

"Right," he groaned. "All the answers."

She settled back in her seat wearing a satisfied smile as he shifted into reverse and prepared to back out of the driveway.

Suddenly Kelsey jerked around in her seat. "Ben! Look! Isn't that the same florist's van from yesterday?"

Ben slammed the car into Park and jumped out, meeting the startled deliveryman halfway up the walk. The hapless driver's expression was bewildered when Ben snatched the single rose out of his hand and crushed it under his heel.

Chapter Ten

Ben was quiet, seemingly absorbed in his thoughts as he drove Kelsey back to the agency. When he pulled the car up in front of her building, he shut off the engine and turned to her. "I promise you we're going to stop him."

She nodded, averting her eyes from his so that he couldn't see the doubts she felt eating away at her. Though she longed to believe Ben, to accept his assurances, something deep inside her warned that it might already be too late. Like a rattler shaking his tail, each rose she received was the killer's deadly warning.

And while she and Ben ran around in circles trying to trap a loan shark, a murderer who had already killed three times was still free, still stalking her.

Theresa Youngblood had received two roses, Shannon, three. Four roses had been delivered to the young woman in St. Louis during the last days of her life. Was Kelsey number five? She'd already received two roses. What number had she been assigned on the killer's hit list? How many days before he struck again? Would the final roses be delivered today? Tomorrow? She shook her head, trying to clear her mind, reminding herself that panic was her worst enemy.

"Ben, what else did you find out about the victim in St. Louis? Did the police report come in last night after I left?"

He shook his head. "No, and we didn't have any more information when I left the office this morning, but I'll check when I get back."

She reached for the door handle and he stopped her with a hand on her arm.

"Will you be all right? Do you want to come with me?"

The thought of spending the rest of the day with Ben was tempting, but Kelsey's sense of duty was stronger. "I've still got an agency to run, remember? And right now I think keeping busy might be exactly what I need."

"We're going to get through this," he said, tilting her chin with one gentle fingertip so that she had to look at him. "Together." He smiled as he leaned over and planted a kiss firmly on her lips to seal his promise. "With two of Chicago's top investigators on the case, how can we go wrong?"

AFTER ACCEPTING Kelsey's thanks, Izzy left about three. At four, Francine explained that she had to leave in order to catch the bus to make the necessary connection to get to her suburban home. Kelsey thanked the young woman for the efficient job of reorganization that she and Izzy had accomplished in just one day.

"Would you like me to come back tomorrow?" Francine asked, reaching for her purse.

"Of course," Kelsey replied. "And if you think you'd like it here, maybe we could discuss a full-time position."

A ready smile split the young woman's face. "That sounds great. I'll see you tomorrow, Ms. St. James."

Kelsey watched the door close behind Francine before she walked into her own office. After a moment alone in the uneasy silence, she walked back into the outer office and locked the door.

For the next two hours, Kelsey tried with little success to concentrate on the McIntire case, a new client she'd taken on last week, involving a young man who was trying to locate his birth parents. But no matter how long she stared, the words on the paper might as well have been written in Greek for all the meaning they held for Kelsey. Her heart and mind were overflowing with her own apprehensions, and try as she might, there was just no room for anything else.

Tonight's plan to trap Roger McElroy and the loan shark loomed as a dark and ominous obstacle that shadowed her every conscious thought. Her stomach churned as she considered the potential for failure at every turn: what if Roger somehow discovered Ben was following him? What if he wouldn't or couldn't reveal the killer's identity before Ben sprung his trap? What if something happened and they were unable to replace the money that Kelsey instinctively knew Ben's career was riding on? What if their plan backfired and Ben was hurt or killed?

That last thought hit her like a physical blow and a stab of breath-robbing pain sliced through her. She forced her thoughts away from that morbid possibility. Losing Ben was unthinkable.

Everything would work out the way they'd planned, she tried to convince herself. Roger would lead them to the loan shark, and to cut a deal and save their own slimy hides, Roger and his back-street associate would reveal the murderer's name.

Ben knew what he was doing. He was a smart cop. Kelsey reminded herself that she, too, was a competent and trained investigator. They weren't amateurs playing cops and robbers but professionals playing for keeps.

Kelsey slid the McIntire papers back into the file cabinet and glanced at the clock on the wall above the door. It was nearly six. Surely by now Ben had received more information from the police department in St. Louis. She picked up the phone and punched in the number, picturing the precinct offices in her mind as the phone rang. Regardless of the hour, homicide always seemed to hum with an undercurrent of tension.

"Detective Tanner's desk," a male voice announced before the third ring. Kelsey recognized the voice as Gil's.

"It's Kelsey St. James, Gil. Is he in?"

"Ah, no, I don't think he is," Gil stammered uneasily. "He stepped out. Had to pick up a package in another part of the building, I think."

The turbulence in her stomach began in earnest. The package Gil referred to had to be the money she would soon be handing over to Roger McElroy.

"He said if you called to tell you he'd meet you later tonight at your place," Gil informed her.

"Have you received any more information on the murder in St. Louis?"

"Hang on. Let me get the paperwork."

Gil was gone for what seemed like an inordinate amount of time. For a moment, Kelsey thought they'd been disconnected and she was about to hang up and redial when he came back on the line.

"Here it is, Kelsey," he said. "It was just coming in over the fax. I haven't read it all, but from what I've gathered, it isn't a very pretty scenario. Are you ready?"

Kelsey took a deep breath and grabbed a pencil and a blank writing pad. "Go ahead, Gil."

"It happened Monday night." The night of Shannon's funeral, Kelsey realized with a shudder. "The victim was pushed through a stairwell at the law office where she worked. The fall killed her outright, but there was some evidence that she was near suffocation before she fell. The composition of the remnants of adhesive found around her mouth matched that found on Shannon's mouth. Her name was White, Jennifer White, age twenty-seven."

Kelsey gasped.

"Are you still there?" Gil asked.

"Yes, yes. I'm here. It's just that name... it sounds so familiar to me."

"Jennifer's a pretty common name," Gill said flatly. "And White's not unusual, either."

Kelsey searched her memory. "You're right. But I'm fairly certain I've met someone by that name." But where and when Kelsey didn't have a clue.

"One of your clients, maybe?" Gil suggested.

"Maybe. I don't know." Kelsey ran her fingers idly through her hair as she thought. "Maybe it will come to me later. Is there anything else, Gil?"

"No, not much that you don't already know. Four roses were found in her office. The card read the same as the one found in your friend's apartment, 'Next in line,' whatever that means. Two ballet tickets were found in her mailbox. No return address."

Kelsey's palms were sweating. "Does the report mention anything about Jennifer's background, where she was born, if she was single or married, that sort of thing?"

"She was single. Birthplace, Illinois. That looks like about all we have for now. Before he left, Ben talked with the chief of homicide in St. Louis. We should be receiving a more detailed report in the next day or so."

"Thanks, Gil," Kelsey said.

"Oh, there was one other thing you might be interested in knowing, something that came in from the FBI this afternoon. Evidently a scrap of adhesive was found at the crime scene in South Carolina. They've identified it as moleskin."

"The stuff people use for bunions, calluses, that sort of thing?" Kelsey asked.

"Yes," Gil answered. "It can be used for those things, or to keep new shoes from slipping. But it's also used by ballerinas," Gil informed her. "Did you know that?"

"No," Kelsey replied. "No, I didn't."

"They cover the tips of their pointe shoes with moleskin to keep from slipping. 'Course I'd have never known about that, either," Gil added quickly, "but those investigators down at Quantico check every angle."

"It seems they're very thorough," Kelsey agreed. "Gil, has the FBI been able to find a connection between the three women yet?" Kelsey asked as she jotted the words "moleskin" and "ballet tickets" on the notepad beside the phone.

"Not yet," Gil replied. "Personally, I think they're stymied. You know, Kelsey," Gil confided, "between you and me, I don't think they're even close. This guy is smart. Cunning. A real professional." Kelsey was stunned by the note of respect she detected in Gil's voice.

"Every time we think we have a focus, he jumbles the picture. He scatters the evidence, jumps from town to town. Sometimes his actions appear almost random. But don't you believe it, Kelsey. Everything he does is planned, right down to the last detail. Everything's calculated. Everything's connected." Gil's grim pronouncements sent a shiver of fresh fear skating through Kelsey's mind.

By what bizarre connection had the murderer linked Shannon Hughes, Theresa Youngblood and Jennifer White? How had he chosen them to be his victims? Had it been their hair color, their taste in clothes, the fact that they were all single? What was it that had drawn him to them? And what was it that Kelsey had in common with all three that marked her as his next victim? she wondered desperately.

When Gil spoke again, the sound of his voice jerked her away from her grisly speculations. "Listen, Kelsey, if there's nothing else I can do for you, I need to get going. I've got a date tonight."

"Of course," Kelsey said quickly. "I'll let you go." She was as eager to end this disconcerting conversation as he was to begin his evening. "Thanks for the information, Gil."

"Sure thing," he said easily. "And if I see Ben on the way out, I'll tell him you called."

Kelsey sat for a long moment after she hung up the phone, wondering why her conversation with Gil Montoya had left her feeling unnerved and angry. Something about his attitude toward this case disturbed her. The things he'd said and the way he'd said them seemed so callous, so cavalier.

Thinking back over his comments, Kelsey was left with the impression that Gil thought of this case as some sort of game, with the outcome determined by the side that proved to be the most cunning. In a way he seemed almost a dispassionate observer. She realized that it was that cold objectivity contrasted with Ben's intense level of commitment that offended her most.

She stood up and walked over to the window and stared out onto the street. She was just having an attack of nerves, she tried to tell herself. In order to function effectively under the difficult circumstances of dealing with Roger and his so-called client, she needed to clear her mind and get a handle on the anger she felt toward the young policeman she barely knew.

Comparing Gil to Ben was as unfair as comparing Ben to her father, she told herself. Cops weren't all the same. Hadn't the past few days of getting to know and respect Ben Tanner taught her at least that much?

But cops were a different breed, she reminded herself, especially those assigned to homicide. The very nature of the crimes they investigated made it imperative for them to maintain an emotional distance, but how they went about achieving that distance was a very personal matter.

For her father, it had been a dedication to rules and regulations. For some, she knew that working out at the gym or participation in some kind of team sport offered a release. For Gil, viewing each case as a puzzle, a game of strategy was probably what helped him achieve a workable distance. Kelsey reminded herself that, even in her own profession, she found she often needed to keep an arm's length from many of the emotionally charged situations that came to her.

And how did Ben Tanner keep his sanity under the pressure, Kelsey wondered. Clearly she was the exception when it came to his personal involvement with his work—and despite the grim circumstances of that involvement, Kelsey smiled. So how did Ben achieve a balance between his life as a police detective and his personal life?

The answer came to Kelsey in a flash of insight: Ben Tanner made his own rules, followed his own instincts. His loyalty was bound not merely to a badge but to the principles it represented. A set of rules, predetermined and prescribed for every situation, would never dictate what course he would follow. To Ben, the line between his professional and personal identity would never be blurred. He was his own man first, a cop second. Kelsey's realization caused her admiration for him to deepen.

With a sigh, she dropped down into her chair again, the animosity she'd felt for Gil Montoya dissolving as she picked up her pen, bent over her desk and wrote down three names on the notepad beside the phone: "Jennifer White. Shannon Hughes. Theresa Youngblood."

What connection existed between the three women? she asked herself for the hundredth time. Would anyone besides the murderer ever know what it was that linked these three strangers whose only obvious similarity was murder?

BEN STOOD outside the evidence room and made conversation with the heavyset officer in charge. Gene Riley was a cop getting close to retirement. Even in his prime he'd been lazy, a cop who complained about everything. Tonight, as he pressed his fleshy face close to the wire mesh of the receiving window, he was confiding to Ben what a raw deal he'd been dealt by being assigned for the past three years to the evidence room.

When the phone rang, Ben forced himself not to react. He knew the voice on the other end of the line would be Gil's, but he feigned ignorance when Gene muttered a colorful curse as he hung up the receiver and turned to Ben, complaining, "It's always something, ain't it?" he moaned. "Now they say my locker's been busted into! Can you believe it? In a police station, for God's sake."

"Would you like me to run up there and take a look, Gene?" Ben offered, betting heavily he'd refuse. It was well-known that Gene Riley used every excuse to escape the confines of the evidence room.

"No, it's okay. But, hey, you could do me a favor if you've got a minute."

Ben glanced down at his watch and frowned, shaking his head slowly. "Well, if it won't take to long, I guess I could. Sure, what do you need?"

Officer Riley shoved his keys into the lock and swung the door open. "Just sit in the cage for a couple of minutes while I run up and check on my stuff. Anybody wants to check something in, take it and tell 'em I'll write it up later. Hey, thanks, man. I owe you.''

"Are you sure it's all right for me to be back here?" Ben hesitated for effect.

"Sure. You're homicide, for God's sake. If Chicago PD can't trust you, who the hell can they trust?"

"Good question," Ben said with a laugh, his mind already picturing the stack of bills he intended to remove from the safe he saw standing partly open at the back of the evidence room. But when it came right down to it, when he was alone with that big bundle of drug money, would he really be able to take it, he asked himself. He was a police officer, sworn to uphold the law, not break it.

A picture of Kelsey's face formed in his mind's eye, and at that moment Ben knew without question that he had no choice. He knew he'd do whatever he had to do to protect her. For Kelsey St. James, the woman who'd taken sole possession of his heart, Ben would do anything.

It was after six when the tall man standing at the florist's counter scrawled his message quickly on the back of the card and slid it across to the white-haired clerk. He'd driven across town to the Jan's House of Flowers farthest from the one Kelsey St. James and Ben Tanner had visited.

"Now that's two long-stemmed red roses, correct?" the clerk asked him.

"Correct," he replied pleasantly. That would send them into a tailspin, he told himself. Their panic would rise with this unexpected change in his operations. They would assume that he'd accelerated his schedule, but they'd be wrong. He was right on track. It had been his plan from the beginning to speed things up with the last two, to change his pace, to move much more quickly, keeping those who thought they could trap him off-balance and confused.

By now they thought they could predict his behavior, but they were fools. They were moving to the beat he'd established as surely as if he'd placed a metronome inside their minds.

The clerk gave him the total, adding an apology for the ten-dollar-extra delivery charge. "But you did say they had to be delivered tonight, correct?"

He smiled as he reached for his wallet. He could see that the clerk was disconcerted by his sunglasses. Strangers were often irritated by the barriers he erected to keep them at bay, but he didn't care.

"And this is the address where you want them delivered, right?" She kept staring at him, squinting a little as though trying to penetrate the tinted glass and catch a glimpse of his eyes. Her lack of manners irritated him.

He gave her the money. "Did you know that if you stare directly into a dog's eyes long enough you'll eventually drive him mad?" he asked her in a tone intentionally casual.

"Why... why, no," she sputtered, averting her gaze immediately. "I've never heard of such an awful thing." He smiled to himself. He'd shaken the old biddy up and he was glad.

She took the money and turned around briskly to get his change from the cash drawer behind her, but by the time she turned again, the strange man in the dark glasses had gone.

KELSEY HAD SEARCHED through her files before leaving the office. The name Jennifer White stuck in her mind, but it was not to be found on any of the case files in her newly reorganized cabinet. About seven, she gave up. Perhaps Gil Montoya was right. The name Jennifer certainly wasn't an uncommon one. And so, with an anxious mind and a heavy heart, Kelsey locked up the agency, hailed a cab and headed home.

Half an hour later, when Kelsey opened her front door, Sherlock and Mr. Chan greeted her enthusiastically.

"Hang on, fellas," she scolded them as she made her way into the kitchen and filled their bowls with food and water. Dolly crept in through the doggy door and cautiously sidled up to Kelsey.

"Well, hello, little one," Kelsey murmured. "Looks like you've been checking out the neighborhood. Ready for dinner?" Dolly's response was a brittle mew. Miss Marple remained regally relaxed on a kitchen chair, watching with wise, disinterested eyes.

On her way to the refrigerator, Kelsey reached over and ran one hand lovingly over Miss Marple's satiny black coat. "You're going to have to share your bowl for a couple more days, Missy." Dolly still wouldn't eat out of the new stainless steel bowl Kelsey had purchased for her.

With her animals fed and watered, Kelsey grabbed a diet soda out of the refrigerator and walked into her bedroom, unbuttoning her blouse and slipping out of her skirt as she walked.

After showering and changing into jeans and a pink T-shirt, she walked back into the living room and checked her answering machine for messages. There was only one, a message from Ben saying he'd be over before eight. She glanced at the clock, and anticipation skittered through her. Thoughts of the dangerous situation she'd soon be facing were blurred by the happiness she felt when she thought of being in his arms again.

She took a sip of her soda and plopped down on the couch. "Jennifer White," she muttered, letting her head fall back on the cushions and her eyes drift closed. "Who were you and why do I think I knew you?"

The sound of sharp barking drew Kelsey back into the kitchen. "What is it, boy?" she asked as she peered out the back window. Sherlock wasn't the kind of dog to bark at shadows, but Kelsey couldn't see anything out of the ordinary in the backyard.

A light tapping sound at the kitchen door sent Sherlock into another fit of loud barking. "Hush," Kelsey ordered as she padded over to the door and opened it. At the sight of Ben standing in her doorway, Kelsey felt her heart roll over.

"What are you doing coming in this way?" she asked him as she stood back and let him step into the kitchen.

"I parked a few blocks over and cut through the neighborhood. I didn't want my car to be seen parked in front of your house in case McElroy decided to drive by to see if you'd complied with his instructions."

Roger's warning to stay away from the police rang in Kelsey's ears. "I'm glad you're here," she said.

He followed her into the living room. "I spoke with Gil before I left. He said you'd called and that he told you about Jennifer White."

Kelsey frowned. "He told me you had gone to pick up a package. Does that mean what I think it does—that you have the money?"

Slowly Ben unbuttoned his faded denim shirt and withdrew a bulky package tucked into the waistband of his jeans. Kelsey couldn't help but notice his broad chest and firm, flat torso that tapered down to a trim waist. A trail of raised, unnaturally white skin defined a scar six inches long that cut a jagged path upward from his rib cage before disappearing into the dusting of springy black hair that covered his chest.

A V of black began again just above the waistband of his jeans. Kelsey had an impulsive urge to touch his warm, tanned body, to know what it would feel like to press her own naked torso against his. She longed to trail her kisses across his skin, to feel the spark of desire his warmth would ignite inside her.

He caught her staring and smiled as he reached for her, pulling her against his hot, dry skin. Her breath caught in her throat as he enfolded her in his arms and kissed her hungrily.

There was nothing tentative or questioning about his caresses. His lips sought hers again and again. Her fingers slid through the hair at his nape and pressed him closer. As their breath mingled, she slid a few inches away from him and slid her hands slowly over his torso, her fingers inching into the black mat of hair on his chest. He uttered a low moan of pleasure at her touch.

When she felt the corded outline of his scar, she jerked her hand away and gasped. "I'm sorry," she cried breathlessly.

He took her hands in his and brought them to his lips. "It doesn't hurt anymore."

"Are you sure?"

He touched her cheek and she looked up at him. His eyes were smoky with desire. "I'm sure." When he moved his lips over hers again, his kiss was so tender, so loving that Kelsey felt as though her heart might burst with the rush of love that filled it.

Without warning, Sherlock's sudden yelp ripped them apart like an invisible hand. "What is it?" Kelsey demanded, whirling around breathlessly to confront the large dog. But Sherlock was oblivious to her scolding. He bolted past her, through the living room, stopping at the front door, where his barking became more frantic.

"Someone's out there," Kelsey said.

Ben buttoned his shirt as he moved quickly into the living room and cautiously inched the curtain open at the side of the window in order to survey the front yard without being seen. "I don't see anything," he said.

Kelsey was peering through the peephole in the front door. "I can't see anything, either. The street is practically deserted."

"Go lie down, Sherlock," Kelsey ordered. "Thatta boy," she praised him when the dog trotted back into the kitchen and curled up on the braided rug in front of the sink.

"He's been acting jumpy all week," she explained as she walked back into the living room where Ben was studying the notes she'd brought home from the office. "Sometimes I think my animals pick up on my moods."

He nodded and handed her the notepad. "Did you come to any conclusions?" he asked.

She shrugged and sat down on the couch, resting her elbows on her knees. "Only that all three women were approximately the same age and single. All born in Illinois."

Ben sat down beside her. "Unfortunately we don't know that much about Jennifer White's background yet."

Just hearing the name again triggered a nagging feeling of familiarity. "Ben, I know that I've either met Jennifer White or had some past dealings with someone by that name," she said. "But I checked my client files before I came home and didn't find anything. I wished I'd had the chance to look further."

"But if you didn't find her name in your files, where else would you look?"

Kelsey thought a moment. "My Rolodex, maybe. Or the Rolodex in the reception area. Ben, that name is so familiar to me."

Ben glanced at his watch. "It's not even nine," he said. "If we left now we'd have time to drive down to the agency, check your Rolodex and still have you back in plenty of time to catch McElroy's call. If you *have* had some past contact with Jennifer White, we need to do everything to find out what it was."

Kelsey was already on her feet and heading for the front door when Ben stopped her. "Let's go out this way," he said, motioning to the back door.

She followed him into the kitchen. "Watch the house, boy," she ordered as she gave Sherlock an affectionate pat before slipping out the back door with Ben.

IT WAS DARK as they cut through several alleys and jogged three blocks south to where Ben's car was parked. Kelsey's mind worked overtime as they drove, but the connection between herself and Jennifer White remained defiantly at the edge of her memory.

They were only two blocks from the agency when a fire truck, sirens blaring, rushed past them through a red light. "Look at that, Ben," Kelsey said, pointing after the fire truck, "he's turning onto LaSalle."

Ben hit the accelerator, following the emergency vehicle around the corner. The street was alive with lights and sirens. An eerie yellow light reflected off the angry flames that licked through the thick cloud of choking black smoke.

Firemen and uniformed policemen had cordoned off the block and were directing traffic onto a side street. A crowd of people gathered at the end of the block responded with ooos and ahhhs as though they were watching a fireworks display when a series of small explosions shook the night air.

Ben pulled his car up to the last set of barricades, jumped out and jogged over to a fireman manning the blockade. "What's going on?" he asked, pulling his badge from his back pocket and flipping it open for the fireman to see.

"There's been an explosion in that building over there!" The fireman had to shout to be heard over the commotion in the street as Ben stepped over the barricade. "From what the neighbors have told us, the building is used mainly for offices and they were closed for the day. There shouldn't have been anyone inside, and it's a good thing, too, 'cause after the first blast, the place went up like a tinderbox.''

With Ben's help, Kelsey clambered over the barricade, her gaze transfixed by a gigantic mass of black smoke that billowed and churned into the night sky, spewing smoking cinders and fiery ash into the street. Frantically she began ticking off the storefronts and offices that lined LaSalle Street. She stared into the fire, the noxious fumes burning her eyes as she sought to confirm or deny her worst suspicions.

Along with the stench of the acrid smoke, reality settled over her in a bitter haze: the structure being devastated by flames was the building that housed St. James Investigations. Kelsey stared in shock, thinking back to the many nights she'd worked late, sometimes sleeping over in her office as she had just last night.

A scarce twenty-four hours ago she'd slept where now a hellish inferno raged. The thought consumed her as the fire continued to ravage what had been, for the past three years, the center of all her hopes and dreams for the future.

A sudden surge of anger swept through her. "No!" she screamed, but her anguished cry was lost in the deafening roar of the second huge blast.

Chapter Eleven

The blow hit like an invisible fist, knocking Kelsey backward, slamming her to the pavement with brutal force. She gasped, frantic to refill her burning lungs. "Ben!" she screamed, suddenly desperate to find him, to know that he was all right. Smoked blurred her vision and burned her eyes. Confusion reigned all around her.

Suddenly she felt his hands touching hers, helping her to her feet. She looked up into his face and the relief that washed through her made her feel as weak as a baby. "Ben," she cried.

"Kelsey," he murmured, his lips close to her ears as he wrapped his arms around her and held her close. "Are you all right?"

"Yes," she sputtered. "Are you?"

"I'm fine," he assured her.

"What happened?" she asked.

With his arm still around her they moved together behind the barricade. "The fire must have spread to the dry cleaner next door—" His words were cut short by another explosion that rocked the ground and shattered the night air.

A burst of flames and smoke belched out into the street as the front of Discount Cleaners was reduced to smoldering rubble. The fire fighters immediately responded, shifting their assault to the newest blaze that sprang to life inside the store.

Suddenly Kelsey spied what she believed was a piece of blazing debris pinwheeling toward them. She blinked and realized that it was not rubble or flying debris but a person! A man stumbling out of the blazing building, his arms flailing against the flames that licked up his back and swirled around each of his legs.

Without thinking she darted under the barricade and raced toward the screaming figure. With all her strength she knocked the man to the ground and dropped down beside him, frantically rolling him from side to side, trying to smother the flames that had already devoured what appeared to be a long thick coat of some kind.

In the next instant, Ben and a fireman were there, a blanket was wrapped around the man and the flames were extinguished. The cries that came from beneath the blanket tore at Kelsey's heart, and for the first time she realized her own hands were singed.

An ambulance crew appeared and bundled the writhing figure onto a stretcher. Before they carried him away, the blanket parted and Kelsey gasped when she recognized the face of the man whose life she'd just saved.

IN THE WAITING AREA outside the emergency room, a nurse applied a thin coating of cooling salve to Kelsey's right hand and in a few minutes the stinging subsided. When the nurse moved away, Kelsey saw Ben emerging from behind the emergency room's wide double doors. He leaned over and kissed her cheek before sitting down beside her.

"How is he?" Kelsey asked.

"He's in pain, but it could have been a lot worse. That old trench coat probably saved his life."

"Is he conscious? Were you able to talk to him?"

Ben nodded, his expression grim. "He was fully aware when I read him his rights. How are *you?*" he asked, reaching for her hand gently and examining the small blisters that had risen on the back.

"I'm fine," she said, releasing a ragged sigh. "But I still can't believe Roger could do such a thing."

"He confessed to planting the explosives in your office before he passed out. The doctors say he was lucky," Ben said. "His injuries are plenty painful but not severe. They've given him medication to put him out for the night, so we won't be able to talk to him again until morning."

"But why did he do it, Ben?"

He shook his head. "I suspect he was trying to warn you, to let you know his so-called client meant business. They probably wanted to make sure that after you turned the money over to them, you'd be too frightened to go to the police."

"What happens now? What about Cecil? What about Shannon's murderer? Do you think Roger ever intended to reveal his identity?"

Ben frowned. "I wish I had all those answers," he sighed. "But for now I guess we have to wait and see if Roger is willing to strike a deal with the DA. There's no doubt he'll be indicted for arson, but as far as proving his involvement with loan sharking and extortion, it's merely your word against his. I spoke with Gil and we've contacted Cecil. At this moment he's in protective custody in Los Angeles. They won't hold him long, but at least long enough for us to work on Roger and his lawyer. Cecil will be safe."

"His lawyer?"

"Vanessa Overholt. She arrived almost before the ambulance."

"But what about Shannon's murderer? Do you really think Roger or his client ever truly intended to name him?"

"I don't know," Ben said, but his expression was doubtful. "Everything about the murders points to a serial killer. Personally, I can't believe that Roger's loan-sharking client had anything to do with Shannon's death or the deaths of Theresa Youngblood or Jennifer White."

There was that name again. "I guess we'll never know if Jennifer White's name was on my Rolodex," Kelsey said wistfully, leaning her head back against the wall and closing her eyes.

Ben's fingers grazed her forehead lightly as he brushed back a lock of hair that had tumbled onto her face. "We'll just have to look somewhere else for the connection."

She opened her eyes to see him studying her face.

"I must look a mighty mess," she groaned.

"You looked mighty good to me, lady," he murmured. His sooty gray eyes, soft and assuring, sent a wave of tenderness rippling through her. "You must be exhausted," he said, taking her uninjured hand. "Let's get you home."

Kelsey nodded. Home was exactly where she wanted to be. Every bone in her body ached. The burns on her hand stung, her knees and her elbows felt scraped and raw where she'd fallen to the ground with Roger. Right now a shower, a cup of herbal tea and her own bed sounded like heaven.

FIFTEEN MINUTES LATER, Kelsey was tugged out of a restless sleep by Ben's touch. "You're home, sleeping beauty," he said, opening the car door and taking her hand as she climbed out of the car. "Give me your keys. I'll unlock the door."

Momentarily forgetting the blisters on her hand, Kelsey reached into her purse. When her injured hand scraped the inside of her bag, she gasped. Ben's brows drew together in a concerned frown.

"The nurse said as soon as the blisters burst, my hand will feel much better," she assured him. "She called me lucky."

Ben was silent as they moved up the walk together. At the door he stopped and turned to her. "I'm the one who's lucky," he declared, pulling her gently into his arms. "When I saw you running toward that burning building, I thought my heart would stop. I don't want to lose you, Kelsey."

His words went straight to her heart, and she smiled and traced with one gentle fingertip the troubled frown that creased his handsome face. Once again his special blend of strength and gentleness had touched her.

"I mean it, Kelsey," he murmured as he pulled her closer. "I wonder if you know just how much you've come to mean to me."

"I know," she whispered, snuggling deeper into his embrace. "Believe me, I know." Her heart almost ached with the love she felt for him. She slid her arms around his neck and drew his face to hers. "I know just how you feel," she whispered again, "because I feel it, too."

He moaned softly when she kissed him. Within the circle of his arms, Kelsey felt safe, invulnerable, almost giddy with happiness.

But without warning Kelsey's euphoria vanished when she glanced down and saw the gold foil florist box waiting for her on the doorstep. With hands trembling and heart racing, she picked up the long, slim package and pulled back the lid. She held her breath as she peeled the white tissue back to reveal two long-stemmed roses. Every illusion of safety shattered around her. "Two roses!" she cried, her voice merely a ragged whisper.

Ben said nothing when he took the florist's box away from her and walked into the house. Without a word he set the roses on the table. Kelsey took a deep breath and reached into the box. Aside from the long-stemmed roses, the only thing she found inside was a blank card with Jan's House of Flowers stamped on the back.

"Two and two makes four," she murmured, her eyes glistening. "He's sent me four roses. That means I've only one more rose to go." How long had Jennifer White, Theresa Youngblood and Shannon had to wait for the final deadly rose to be delivered? she wondered. And what about the ballet tickets? Were they delivered by courier, as well? Or were they left behind by the killer himself, as a kind of grim calling card?

"Gil was right," Kelsey said, her voice shaking. "The murderer is trying to make us think he's acting randomly, breaking his pattern by sending two roses instead of one, but he's still following his plan, Ben. The plan he's detailed right down to the last moment. My last moment." Kelsey shivered, gooseflesh prickling up her arms and the back of her neck.

"When will my last rose arrive, Ben?" she asked, her voice thin and edged with desperation. "How much longer do I have before he comes for me?"

"Please don't talk like that," Ben ordered gently as he put his arm around her and urged her into the living room. "And for God's sake, forget whatever it was that Gil told you. He's a rookie, at least to homicide. This is his first big case. You have all the time in the world, Kelsey. I promise. I won't let anything happen to you."

She stared into his eyes, longing to believe him. "But how—"

"We'll stop him, Kelsey. He's not invincible. He'll make a mistake and when he does we'll catch him. The FBI has assigned two full-time researchers to the case. Did Gil tell you that?"

Kelsey shook her head. She could see that Ben was fighting his irritation with the young officer he'd been assigned to mentor.

"We'll stop him, sweetheart," Ben promised, and when his arms closed around her, Kelsey buried her face against his chest, willing herself to believe him.

In a moment he said, "It's nearly midnight. You must be exhausted. Let me fix you a cup of tea, and then you need to get some rest."

She offered him a weak smile as he walked into the kitchen and put the kettle on the stove. When he came back into the living room and sat down beside her, she said, "I doubt that I'll sleep much tonight. We need to keep trying to find the connection between Shannon, Jennifer and Theresa. I've got my notes right here." But before she could reach the yellow tablet lying on the table beside them, he grabbed her hand.

"What's the matter?" she asked, sliding her hand out of his grasp.

"No more work tonight, Kelsey," he said evenly. "Tonight you need to rest."

"But how can I rest?" she demanded to know. "We've lost whatever lead we might have had with Roger. Now more than ever we've got to find the connection, Ben. You said it yourself—the best chance we have to stop Shannon's killer is to study his victims. Well, I was not only a friend of one of his victims, but now I'm his victim, as well." Her emotional comments were punctuated by the teakettle's sudden scream as the water inside erupted into a burst of steam.

Kelsey jumped and Dolly, who had been curled up sleeping in the easy chair by the window, arched to life, leaping out of the chair as though she'd been charged with a sudden jolt of electricity.

As the frightened kitten sprang out of the chair and skittered across the room, she upended the box of photographs sitting on top of Shannon's cedar chest.

Ben rose and hurried into the kitchen, where he proceeded to fix a pot of tea while Kelsey gathered the pictures and papers that had fallen to the floor. She was oblivious to his movements when he brought their tea into the living room and set the cups down on the coffee table in front of the couch.

Kelsey sat transfixed by the picture she held in her hand, the photograph she'd shown Ben the day after Shannon's funeral, the picture of her second-grade dance recital.

"What is it?" Ben asked, sitting down beside her. "Is something wrong?"

"Oh, Ben," she cried, sudden and sickening realization dawning. "Oh, my God! This is it. The connection. It's been right under my nose all along."

His gaze traveled from her face to the photograph. He took the picture from her and stared at it. "What do you see, Kelsey?"

"There," she said, pointing at the little girl in pigtails standing on the other side of Shannon. "It's her. Jennifer White!" Her voice was shrill with emotion.

Ben's eyes narrowed. "Jennifer White was in your second-grade dance class?"

"Yes," she cried. "With Shannon and me."

"Are you telling me that two of the women who are in this photograph have been murdered?" His face was a mask of disbelief. "That's incredible!"

"But it's true, Ben. Don't you see? It's the connection we've been searching for." An odd mix of triumph and despair filled her.

"What about Theresa Youngblood? Is she in this picture? Did you know her, as well?" Ben asked, handing the photograph back to Kelsey.

She studied the picture again, shaking her head uncertainly. "She might be," she said slowly. "But her name doesn't ring a bell. Let's see . . . let me think."

Dredging her memory, Kelsey thought about the girls in the dance class, some of whom she hadn't seen in more than twenty years. "There was Shannon and Jennifer..."

"Who's this?" Ben interrupted, pointing to the little girl to the left of Jennifer White. "I think her name was Terri something." She thought a moment.

"That's right. I'm sure her name was Terri. But I can't seem to remember her last name. It was so long ago...her name was Terri, Terri—"

"Wait a minute," Ben said. "Kelsey, couldn't Terri have been shortened from Theresa?"

She felt a cold hand close around her heart. "Of course it could," she gasped. "Ben, didn't the FBI report say that Theresa Youngblood was married?"

"That's right. Youngblood must have been Theresa's married name."

"No wonder her name didn't ring any bells," Kelsey said. "Can we find out what her maiden name was?"

Before she had even finished her sentence, Ben was reaching for the phone. He dialed the precinct quickly, barking out his request. As he waited for an answer, he stared over Kelsey's shoulder at the photograph.

"Who's that?" he asked. "The little star with the roses?"

She opened her mouth to answer, but he raised a hand to stop her, indicating that someone had come back on the line. Kelsey held her breath.

A second later, Ben covered the receiver with his palm and said, "Parker. Is the little girl in that picture Terri Parker?"

Kelsey felt as if she were falling. "Yes," she replied solemnly. Theresa Youngblood and Terri Parker were one and the same.

Ben hung up the phone and sat down beside her and put his arms around her. Neither of them said anything for several minutes.

Finally Kelsey stirred. "It all makes sense now, doesn't it, Ben?" she said quietly. "I'm the last in line." She picked up the picture again. "See?" She pointed. "My costume has five white dots. Jennifer's has four. Shannon's three and Terri's two. At the end of the dance, we'd all fall down. Just like dominoes, one falls and they all fall." Her words carried a ring of desperation as the song came back to her, its simple tune playing over and over in her mind. *"One fall down. All fall down. Each little domino tumble to the ground."* Imagining the mind that had twisted the innocent meaning of a child's song into something so perverse, so deadly, made Kelsey feel hopelessly afraid and weak.

"What about the little girl who was first in line?" Ben asked quietly. "Who is she? Do you remember her, Kelsey?"

She left his arms reluctantly to study the picture again. "Her name was Deirdre Merriweather. Miss Claire, our dance instructor, was her mother. Deirdre was always the star of our class," she explained with a wistful smile. "She was the prettiest, the only one with real talent."

"Where is she now, Kelsey? Do you know what became of her?"

The implication of Ben's questions hit her full force. Deirdre Merriweather had been domino number one.

Had she been the killer's first victim? Her hands flew to her mouth and she stifled a sob. "Oh, Ben, you don't think..."

He shook his head. "I don't want to make any guesses. But we've got to try to contact her, to warn her. Do you know where she is now?"

Kelsey took a sip of tea, trying to clear her overworked and overwrought senses. "I remember that Deirdre didn't go to public school with the rest of us, so we weren't exactly what you would call friends. I never saw Deirdre except at our Saturday dance classes and during rehearsals and recitals. Miss Claire was a widow and she doted on her only daughter night and day, pushing Deirdre to excel long after the rest of us had dropped out of our dance classes.

"Deirdre went on to become something of a local star. By the time she was eight, she'd appeared on every local TV station. When she was thirteen or fourteen I heard she'd traveled to Europe to audition for an international ballet company."

"If she's a famous dancer, she shouldn't be too difficult to locate."

"But that's just it, I don't know if she ever made the big time. I don't even know if she made it out of Willowbend. Unfortunately I can't remember ever hearing anything more about her after the rumors of her European trip."

"Does her mother still live in Willowbend?"

"I have no idea," Kelsey said as she reached for the phone. "But there's one quick way to find out."

By calling information, Kelsey learned that the number for Claire Merriweather had been disconnected, but a number for Miss Claire's School of Dance was still listed. Kelsey dialed the number quickly.

"Kelsey, hang up," Ben ordered gently. "It's after midnight. No one is going to answer at the dance studio at this hour."

Reluctantly she hung up the phone. With a discouraged sigh, she sank back down onto the couch beside him, letting her head fall back onto the cushions and closing her eyes.

"I think we've done all we can for tonight," he said as he began to gently massage her neck and shoulders. "You're exhausted. You need to sleep. I'll stay here tonight. You'll be safe. Tomorrow I'll contact the police in Willowbend and give them the information about Deirdre Merriweather and the others."

"I think I'll drive over to Willowbend in the morning," Kelsey said without opening her eyes.

His hand froze on her shoulders. "What?"

"Well, it makes sense, doesn't it? We've finally uncovered the thread that binds the victims together. Now I've got to trace that connection back to its beginning." Kelsey opened her eyes and turned to face him, determination replacing her earlier expression of defeat. "Willowbend is where it all started. I have to know what has happened to Deirdre Merriweather. Who knows, she might still live there. At any rate, I want to talk to her mother. She knew all of us, worked with us when we were children. Maybe she can help me uncover the final connection, the one that leads to the murderer."

Ben's brows knitted together in a frown. "Kelsey, listen to me. First thing tomorrow, I'm placing you under twenty-four-hour police protection. Whoever is tracking you has decided to step up his pace. The fact that he sent two roses proves that he has accelerated his plans," he said. "As of tomorrow, this entire matter, and with all likelihood my investigation, will be under the auspices of the FBI."

She rose and paced a few feet across the room before she turned around to stare at him. The look on her face was disbelieving. "But you said yourself that because of my personal involvement I could see things the experts could miss. What's changed?"

"That personal involvement is exactly what's changed. So long as the killer is still out there, you're in grave danger. You're no longer in the position of hunter, Kelsey."

He followed her when she walked into the kitchen. They stared down at the roses still lying on the kitchen table. The next thing Ben knew, Kelsey had snatched them up and was striding purposefully toward the garbage can beside the back door. "I can't stand the thought of sitting idly by, playing the intimidated victim," she declared as she angrily stuffed the roses in the trash can. "And I can't believe you're asking me to back away from everything now, just when we're so close to an answer."

"Kelsey, this isn't about me asking you to give up anything. Don't you understand? This isn't your own personal problem. It isn't your investigation."

Her eyes snapped an icy blue. "So you're pulling rank on me, is that it?"

He blew out an exasperated breath. "God, you're stubborn."

"And you're ignoring the value I bring to this case. If you ask me, you're the one who's lost your objectivity, Tanner, and I think you know it!'' she snapped, turning her back to him.

He came up behind her, took hold of her shoulders and gently spun her around to face him. Gazing into the eyes that made him feel weak with desire, he was torn between the urge to shake her or kiss her senseless. "You could be right," he growled, "but at least I realize the risks involved. And whether you like it or not, I'm still the investigator assigned to this case, Kelsey. This *is* an official police investigation, remember? We're not dealing with a runaway wife or a fraudulent insurance claim. I have a job to do and I intend to do it."

Her look of cold resentment stabbed him, but he went on. "There are ways of dealing with monsters like the one who's stalking you. There are procedures, techniques, proven methods—"

"Professional methods?" she blurted out. "As opposed to the amateur techniques used by PIs like me. Isn't that what you're trying to say, Tanner?"

When she jerked out of his grasp, he started to reach for her hand but decided against it. "Kelsey, listen to me," he ordered quietly, fighting to maintain his patience. "You don't have to prove anything. Not to me. Not to anyone. I respect you as a professional, you know that. You've built a successful agency. You've proven you can do the job your father said you couldn't."

She glared at him, but he charged ahead. "Forgive him, Kelsey. Forgive yourself. Do whatever it is you have to do to get on with your life. For your own sake. For our sake."

He could almost feel the anger and hurt churning inside her as his own heart thudded heavily against his chest. He'd gone too far by mentioning her father, he told himself. But he'd felt he had no choice. If by trying to jolt her to her senses he'd created a rift between them that could never be mended, he'd have to learn to live with it. It was better than trying to live with the agony of losing her to a demented killer.

"I think you'd better go," she said, her voice quavering with emotion. "You're right. I need to sleep. There's no need for you to stay. I have a gun and I know how to use it. And I have Sherlock to warn me."

He took a step toward her, but she backed away from him.

"Don't do this, Kelsey," he warned her. "You know how I feel about you. How you feel about me."

She jutted her chin defiantly and stared up at him, her magnificent blue eyes shimmering with the emotions that battered her. "Then prove it," she demanded. "Trust me. Trust my instincts. Go with me tomorrow to Willowbend."

"You know I can't do that," he said. Tomorrow morning he had to replace the money he'd taken from the evidence room. Then he planned to be the first thing Roger McElroy saw when he opened his eyes. "If McElroy knows the identity of the man who murdered Shannon Hughes, Theresa Youngblood and Jennifer White—the man who's planning to murder *you*—then I've got to be there to get that information. I'm a cop, Kelsey. I've got a job to do. I can't go running off halfway across the state on a hunch. Surely you can understand that."

Her gaze fell away from his. He could see the emotions tugging her. It was the same turmoil he felt tearing at his own heart.

"I do understand," she said finally, turning and walking slowly to the front door. "I understand completely. Once a cop, always a cop. Duty first, right, Detective?"

He felt his own anger rising. "It's what I am," he replied without apology.

She opened the door. "Good night, Tanner."

Ben had to fight to control the frustration that was turning to total exasperation. How could a woman so smart, so compassionate and understanding be so totally stubborn, so completely blind to what he could see so well? "Damn it, Kelsey! Don't do this."

"It's late," she said, her voice husky with emotion. "You'd better go."

With a curt nod and his heart in his throat, Ben walked out the door.

By NINE the next morning, Kelsey had showered and dressed. After conversations with the fire department and the owner of the devastated office building, she fed and watered her animals and packed an overnight bag. As an afterthought she called Nelson Masters. He was distraught by news of the fire but assured her that he would do anything he could to assist her in setting up a temporary office.

Kelsey hung up the phone feeling tired, telling herself she wasn't disappointed that Ben hadn't called, that it was the emotional and physical rigors of the previous night that slowed her down and kept her from leaving earlier.

But her heart knew better, and as she tossed her case into the back seat and slid in behind the steering wheel, Kelsey felt empty, alone and completely miserable.

As she drove through her neighborhood, heading for the freeway and the long drive to Willowbend, her thoughts were fastened firmly on Ben. Just over a week ago he'd been a stranger, just another cop. Today he held her heart in his hands. How come she couldn't contemplate life without him? How come everything he'd said and done since the moment they'd met had left an indelible mark on her memory? How had he claimed her heart with his gentle touches, and a couple of kisses? And more important, how could she ever apologize for the awful way she'd treated him last night? And how would he respond when she pulled over at the next exit and called him?

Chapter Twelve

If only she'd been able to speak to Ben, to somehow locate him before leaving Chicago, the drive to Willowbend wouldn't have seemed so miserable. But Ben hadn't been in when she'd phoned the precinct, and according to the officer with whom she'd spoken, no one knew when he'd be back.

For a moment after the line went dead, Kelsey had stood inside the phone booth arguing with herself. She had even considered calling the hospital. No doubt Ben was there, making good on his promise to be there when Roger McElroy regained consciousness. She'd looked up the number in the tattered phone book suspended by a crimped metal chain before she'd decided to drive on to Willowbend and try the precinct number from her motel room.

By the time Kelsey walked into the office of the Discount Ten Motel on the highway outside Willowbend, she felt as if she'd spent the past eight hours in a rain forest. The Chevy's air conditioner had given up all pretence of functioning ten minutes out of Chicago, and thirty miles later the radiator had blown.

The walk hadn't been that long; the next small town had been a little less than two miles from where she'd broken down. But the midday heat and humidity had left her feeling drained, and the three hours spent waiting for her car to be repaired had effectively wasted the better part of the day. Now all she could think about was an air-conditioned room and a cool shower.

What she didn't want or need was the narrowed glances from the gray-haired man behind the check-in counter.

"Traveling alone, are you?" he asked.

"Yes," Kelsey answered as she finished filling out the registration form and slid it and her credit card across the counter to him.

"Staying just the one night?"

She fought for patience, reminding herself that a young woman checking into a hotel or motel alone, an event hardly noteworthy in Chicago, would be viewed as an oddity in a small town like Willowbend.

"Yes," she said, forcing herself to sound pleasant. "Just for tonight." She couldn't help wondering what his reaction might have been had she told him she was in Willowbend to track a serial killer.

Five minutes later, Kelsey pulled her car up to the curb in front of the unit that matched the number on the key the manager had given her. The door opened easily into a room that was small and utilitarian but clean and cool. After pulling a fresh blouse and skirt from her overnight bag and tossing them on the bed, Kelsey undressed.

She hesitated at the phone beside the bed. The chances of catching Ben at his office were slim. The thought of the cool spray that awaited her made her decision final. She'd waited this long to talk to Ben, so she could wait a bit longer, at least until after her shower.

DEIRDRE RARELY KNOCKED before entering any room, and although by now he should have grown accustomed to her blatant disregard for his privacy, he still winced when she walked into his old bedroom.

"Close the drapes," he grumbled. "The sun is blinding me." His room faced west, overlooking the swing set in the backyard.

Deirdre stood basking in the rays that streamed through the smudged window. "Too bad you can't enjoy the sun," she said with mocking sincerity. "I love the sun. Always have." With the light streaming through the window behind her, she was a cutout in black.

"Why did you follow me?" he asked, sliding to a sitting position and reaching for the dark glasses on the table beside the bed. "I thought you hated the country."

"Hated it?" she said incredulously. "Why, wherever did you get that idea?"

"How about the fact that you spent half your life running away to big cities," he shot back bitterly as he eased back onto the pillows and closed his eyes. "Go away, Deirdre. I need to rest."

He felt her moving up beside the bed. "I know something you don't know," she taunted. "About Kelsey St. James."

"I haven't got time for your games." He opened his eyes and tried without success to focus on her face. "If you have something to say, say it."

"She won't be as easy to surprise as the others. She's a very smart lady, you know."

He closed his eyes again. "I agree, she's smart. That's hardly a secret." His head hurt, and his stomach burned from too much coffee and not enough rest. Spending last night watching Kelsey St. James's house had taken a toll on his physical and mental state.

"You're not going to get away with it," she said simply, moving away from the bed. "Your plan won't work on this one."

"You don't know what you're talking about," he shot back, but even as he spoke the doubts her careless comment had planted were already taking seed. Would he ever acquire an immunity to the mental torment she provoked, he wondered miserably.

"And now that she's teamed up with that cop..." Her voice faded, leaving him to draw his own grim conclusions.

The room was hot and the air was stale, but he dared not open a window. The constant churning sound coming from the fan overhead, coupled with Deirdre's taunting, irritated and unnerved him.

"Why don't you give it up," she suggested. "Admit that you're beaten."

"I won't admit anything," he snapped. "Leave me alone, Deirdre. I have work to do tonight. I need to rest."

"That's exactly what I intend to do, brother dear," she said flippantly as she moved closer to the window. "When Kelsey St. James finally puts all the pieces together, they'll come after you and then you'll be alone for a good, long time." She sighed dramatically. "Mother will be devastated, of course. She'll never want to lay eyes on you again once all your dirty little secrets are out in the open."

He swung his legs over the edge of the bed and rose to his full height. "Get out!" he yelled.

"I'm going. I don't want to be here any more than you want me," she said calmly. "But just remember, when they come for you, don't bother calling me. And Mother won't come to you, either—I'll see to that. I'll tell her everything, every stupid secret I ever kept for you. I'll take her away with me. You'll never see her again."

He cursed her under his breath and brought his hands up to massage his temples. "Shut up, Deirdre," he groaned. "Why won't you let me rest?"

She seemed not to have heard. "Mother and I will always be together, no matter what you do. And you, my pathetic brother, will always be alone." She punctuated her words with a sharp laugh. The familiar sound jolted through him, reverberating through his brain, sending pain through his head.

She'd laughed at him in exactly the same way that night in Atlanta. He remembered her taunting him when he ran out onto the balcony to silence her. He remembered the fear in her eyes when he grabbed her, the sound of her screams when she fell. The rush of adrenaline that had given him the power to stifle her cruel laughter then surged through him now. He'd had the power to silence her once and he vowed to do it again.

Everything would work out, he told himself, sinking back down onto the bed, closing his eyes and taking a deep breath to quiet his racing heart. So far everything had gone according to plan.

In a moment the ache behind his eyes began to subside. When he thought about his plan it gave him the strength to continue. It was almost over, he assured himself. With each dancer's death, Deirdre's hold on Mother was loosened a little more.

"All fall down. All fall down..." And soon it would be Deirdre's turn. She would take her final bow. No longer would he be forced to endure her mocking his days and haunting his nights.

Did Deirdre know that on the death of Kelsey St. James, she, too, would be removed once and for all from his life? Could she feel it? He guessed that she could. Sometimes he sensed her quiet desperation. Even now, as he watched her primping before the mirror that hung above the battered dresser, he sensed she knew her time was growing short. Lately, her attempts to distract him, to destroy his confidence, had become more cruel, more desperate. Sometimes she almost seemed afraid.

She had to suspect what he knew for certain—that without her treachery, Mother would turn to him at last, seeing him for the loyal son he'd always been.

He'd killed the others with cold proficiency, without leaving a trace of evidence behind to reveal his identity. And when it was all over, every trace of Deirdre would be eliminated, as well. The fact that his past crimes, that his plans for the future, had gone undetected for so long gave him a feeling of invincibility.

Of course, Deirdre was right about one thing. Kelsey St. James would be his greatest challenge. Perhaps it had been inevitable that she would uncover the connection between herself and the others, that she would feel compelled to make the trip to Willowbend. But what did it matter?

Merely uncovering the connection wouldn't be good enough. She couldn't stop him now. There wasn't time. In the end it would be her own natural instincts, her irrepressible need to know that would prove her undoing. Somehow that irony made his victory even sweeter, satisfying his need for symmetry.

"What are you thinking?" Deirdre demanded to know, jolting him out of his reverie. When he didn't answer, she said, "You're thinking about those locks, aren't you?" She smiled innocently at her reflection in the glass. "About those rooms with the steel doors? I bet you just can't wait to get back."

A familiar rage grew to a deafening roar inside his head as he started toward her. He could almost feel his hands tightening around her fragile neck.

When he was almost upon her, she turned abruptly to face him. The sun's reflection glinting in her eyes nearly blinded him. He whispered her name through clenched teeth.

Deirdre had always been nimble, and when he lunged at her, she sidestepped his attack with the startling quickness of a cat. When he fell, his head hit the dresser. The jarring pain vibrated through his body. Humiliation choked him as he slumped to the floor.

Deirdre left a trail of tinkling laughter as she walked out of the room, closing the door softly behind her, leaving him alone with his hatred and his murderous thoughts.

IT WAS AFTER FIVE when Kelsey swallowed her disappointment at not being able to reach Ben at either his home or the precinct and decided to walk the six blocks from her motel into the heart of downtown Willowbend. The heavy air carried the scents from the river north of town, bringing with it a familiar musky smell that awakened girlhood memories.

She inhaled deeply, remembering the long, sultry days spent on the river, the magical freedom of those muggy summer nights when the house was too hot for sleeping and she and Shannon had been allowed to play outside well past their bedtime.

As Kelsey walked up Fourth Street she found herself hopelessly immersed in gentle reverie. Her gaze wandered to the steeple of the First Methodist Church and she blinked back the bittersweet images that flooded her. Shannon had been a beautiful bride, Kelsey remembered, her heart aching. They said time made one forget, but Kelsey didn't want to forget Shannon, she just wanted the pain to end.

Her eyes scanned the block north of the church for the white clapboard structure that had housed Miss Claire's School of Dance. She walked quickly toward the studio, reminding herself why she had come to Willowbend. When she reached Miss Claire's, Kelsey stood for a moment on the sidewalk in front of the studio and took in the changes in the two-story house she remembered so well.

The most glaring change was the color. The traditional white exterior had been exchanged for a deep Wedgwood blue. With its shudders and trim painted a bright yellow, the stately old house took on a slightly startled expression.

The wooden sign that had hung over the front door for so many years was gone, replaced by a metal sign that read Michael Grady Photography. Immediately her mind conjured a picture of tall, reed-thin Mike Grady. He'd shot all the photos for the school magazines and won prizes in the county art shows for his work. He'd graduated from Willowbend High a couple of years ahead of her and Shannon.

But if Mike Grady lived here now, where was Miss Claire? And perhaps more important, where was Deirdre?

Her questions propelled her across the broad porch and up to the front door. Kelsey pressed the doorbell and listened to its clear tones echo through the narrow wooden hallway that ran beside the stairway. She imagined walking down that hallway, past the two small changing rooms and into the large, bright practice room. With its gleaming hardwood floors and soft pink walls, the big room at the back of the house had been the site of Miss Claire's instruction for a generation of Willowbend's aspiring young dancers.

Kelsey pressed the bell again at the same time she noticed the small hand-lettered sign taped to the corner of the front window announcing the studio's hours. Nine to five on weekdays, ten to three on the weekends. Kelsey glanced at her watch. It was nearly six-thirty. Mike would be gone for the day. Kelsey rang the bell again, although there was nothing to indicate that Mike Grady used the upper floor of the house for his personal residence the way the Merriweathers had.

After waiting only a few moments for a response to the bell, Kelsey stepped down off the porch and glanced up at the second story, where the panes of two small dormer windows were clouded with age and neglect. For a second, as she followed the cement path around the north side of the house, she had the eerie sensation that she was being watched. Attributing the feeling to an overactive imagination and a lack of sleep, Kelsey continued walking toward the back of the house.

The backyard was surrounded by a waist-high picket fence that was badly in need of a fresh coat of white paint. The narrow wooden gate wore a chain and padlock. Kelsey felt a twinge of sadness when she saw how the grass and weeds had overtaken the once-flourishing rose garden that had always been a source of pride for Claire Merriweather.

The swing set at the back of the yard where Miss Claire allowed her students to play after their dance classes stood like a rusting skeleton. The swings themselves and the sliding board, as well as the two-seated metal glider, were gone. A single length of twisted chain swayed dismally from the upper crossbar, the only testament that children had ever played there.

Kelsey's attention was drawn to the swing set's uppermost crossbar. A vague image of a child falling began to emerge from her memory. Strangely, the strains of the domino melody from her first recital accompanied the memory of a crying child and Miss Claire's awful screams.

Kelsey stared at the crossbar without blinking, trying to remember the details. *"One fall down. All fall down."* "Deirdre!" she whispered, suddenly remembering. Deirdre Merriweather had been the child who had fallen. She hadn't really been hurt, but she'd been badly frightened.

Kelsey could still remember the tears that had streaked that small heart-shaped face. Miss Claire had emerged from the house white-faced and visibly shaken.

Kelsey remembered her horror as she'd watched the normally unflappable Miss Claire grab Deirdre's brother and slap him viciously across the face, shoving him into the house while scolding him for failing to watch out for his young sister.

Although Kelsey herself could not have been more than seven or eight, she recognized the look of triumph in Deirdre's small face. The expression in her brother's dark eyes had struck Kelsey, as well. That haunted expression had stayed with her, sending her running to her mother's bed later that night when those dark eyes stared back at her from her troubled dreams.

Other than that day at the swing set, Kelsey couldn't remember ever seeing Deirdre's brother again. Whispers from the Willowbend rumor mill hinted that the boy had been the shame of Miss Claire's life, the product of a youthful and never-discussed relationship between Miss Claire and a well-known choreographer from Spain.

Standing alone at the Merriweathers' back gate, staring into the past, Kelsey felt inexplicably fearful. She turned and walked quickly to the street, telling herself as she walked that the eyes she felt boring into her back were nothing more than childhood memories stirred to life by her own restless imagination.

ON HER WAY BACK to her motel, Kelsey stopped to eat dinner at a café attached to one of the larger motels just up the road from the one where she was staying. The vegetables in her salad were fresh and crisp, the atmosphere in the small café warm and cozy. Yet Kelsey ate without really tasting and glanced with unseeing eyes at the diners around her.

Her mind skittered from one dead end to the next, her frustration mounting. It was almost nine o'clock. The entire day seemed an incredible waste of time—precious time that, if a killer had his way, she didn't have to spare.

Feeling physically and mentally drained, Kelsey made her way back to the motel in the dark. As she walked along, feeling discouraged and lonely, her thoughts drifted to Ben.

During the turmoil of the past several days, his wry humor and gentle understanding had been like a lifeline to a drowning victim. Tonight, in this sleepy little town, far away from everyone who knew or cared for her, she felt her need for Ben more sharply than ever. Did she love him, she asked herself. Was it love that caused her to long for the sound of his voice, the feel of his gentle touch? Was it love when without him Kelsey felt as if she were sinking?

At her room, she slid the key into the lock and pushed the door open. The red message light was blinking on the phone beside the bed. Kelsey's heartbeat quickened as the possibility that Ben might have tried to reach her ignited a flicker of anticipation. Rational thought told her there was no way Ben could have known where she'd be staying, but her hands still trembled as she dialed the manager.

When a gruff male voice growled, "Office," Kelsey said, "This is Ms. St. James in room seven. My message light is on."

"Hold on," the voice ordered over the sounds of a blaring television in the background.

Kelsey reached for a tissue and blotted the moisture from her forehead and throat. As was normal for this time of year, the dark brought no relief from the heat. With her free hand she pulled a can of diet soda from her bag and wondered where the ice machine was located.

A rustling sound came over the line and brought Kelsey's attention back to the receiver. "Looks like somebody left something here for you."

"What? Something for me? But who?" Kelsey's thoughts spun in a dozen different directions at once.

"Don't know. Wasn't on duty when it came."

"But what—"

"If you want to come over and get it, come on," the clerk interrupted impatiently. "We don't have no room service, you know, and the wife and me is gettin' ready for bed."

"Fine," Kelsey answered quickly. "I'll be right over."

"Don't have no extra vases. But the missus says she can loan you a mason jar."

"A vase?" Kelsey asked, her voice tremulous.

"Yeah. In this heat, this here rose is looking mighty sickly. It won't make it much longer without water."

Kelsey gasped and the phone slid from her hand as though it had been dipped in butter.

AFTER QUESTIONING the motel manager and his wife for fifteen frustrating minutes, Kelsey was glad to get back to her room. Neither of them had been in the office when the delivery had been made, and the florist from which the rose had been ordered was closed for the day.

Kelsey considered calling the local police, but dismissed the idea. It was the Chicago Police Department she should contact, and it was one cop in particular with whom she needed to speak.

In the course of the next hour, Kelsey paced an invisible trench through the middle of the room, checked the lock a dozen times and called Ben's precinct twice, only to discover that both Ben and Gil were out of the building. Kelsey reported the delivery of the rose to the officer on duty at the precinct with instructions that he get the message to Ben and to the FBI as soon as possible.

After she hung up, Kelsey sat on the side of the bed feeling numbed. She got up to switch off the air conditioner when the constant humming sound became maddening. But the ensuing silence only seemed to magnify each sound tenfold, and Kelsey's nerves, already taut as piano wires, felt strained to the point of snapping.

Finally the heat and the midnight noises that filled the room forced her to turn the machine on again. For a long moment she stood in front of it, drinking in the cool air.

All right, Kelsey, she told herself with as much calm as she could muster, *you need to look at the situation logically.* Chances were good that the killer was still in the Chicago area. It was chilling to realize that he knew where she was staying, but was that really so incredible? After all, Willowbend wasn't Chicago. There were only four motels in town. Locating the right one would only have taken a couple of phone calls and an innocent inquiry or two. What motel clerk would have de-

nied information to someone wishing to send one of his
guests flowers?

Chances were also good that her stalker had ordered the rose by phone, Kelsey rationalized. She had
planned to contact Mike Grady first thing in the
morning, but a call to the local florist would now pre-
empt that plan.

For now, the question that troubled Kelsey most, the
one for which she could find no ready answer, was how
the killer had known she would be coming to Willowbend in the first place. Was there a bug on her phone
at home? Had he spoken to someone she knew? Both
of those possibilities seemed unlikely. Besides, not
many people knew of her plans to travel to Willowbend. Kelsey mentally ticked off the limited number of
people she had told. Besides Ben, she'd told the fire
investigator to whom she'd spoken before leaving Chicago, the representative from the insurance company
who was handling the claim on the Printer's Row
building, the neighbor she'd asked to look in on her
animals while she was away and Nelson Masters.

Was it possible that one of these was a demented
killer? Or had one of them unknowingly revealed her
plans to the man who stalked her? Both possibilities,
and all the implications that arose from them, seemed
impossibly farfetched.

For the next hour every scenario Kelsey tried to
construct seemed less likely than the next. He could
have followed her, Kelsey admitted to herself at last.
And that was the most likely and the most distinct and
chilling possibility of all.

But what did that mean? That he was out there, even
now, watching her? That he planned to strike while she

was in Willowbend? If that was his plan, Kelsey couldn't help but wonder what had changed his course of action. She'd received the final rose, but what about the tickets? And how did he propose to push her to her death from a ground-floor motel window? An involuntary shudder accompanied that last morbid thought.

But she wasn't defenseless, Kelsey reminded herself. She did have some advantages, like the gun she'd brought with her. She knew how to protect herself. Aside from the self-defense courses she'd completed, she'd begun a class in karate. Also in her favor was the fact that her stalker no longer had the element of complete surprise.

Tonight he'd sent his clearest message, almost as though he'd stepped out of the shadows to declare his final intent. But he'd broken his pattern, and Kelsey couldn't help but wonder if her trip to Willowbend had forced his hand.

She shut off the air conditioner and the lights and sat down on the bed again. The night noises beyond the door crept back into her consciousness. Drawing her knees up to her chest, she wrapped her arms around them and released a shaky breath. All she had to do was get through tonight, she told herself. The clicking and tapping and croaking sounds beyond the door were merely the sounds of life from the river—the cricket, frog and insect sounds that she'd grown up with.

Tonight was similar to those long-ago childhood nights when she'd roamed the streets of Willowbend carefree, with one terrible exception: tonight a killer stalked her.

In his arrogance, he felt he had the upper hand. And in a way he was right, Kelsey admitted. She was afraid.

Hell, she was nearly out of her mind with fear. The night that lay ahead of her was filled with uncertainty and dread.

But there would be a tomorrow, she promised herself resolutely, pulling her gun from her purse and positioning it on the table beside the bed. Tomorrow she would strike out again to find the answers to reveal the killer's identity. Tomorrow she'd be back in Chicago, back in Ben's arms. And if it was the last thing she ever did, in his arms was exactly where she intended to stay.

But for tonight, she was a prisoner of fear. And she had no choice but to wonder and listen and wait for the light.

Chapter Thirteen

Kelsey had no idea what time it was when she was jolted awake. The drapes were drawn, and except for the diffused glow from the neon motel sign on the corner, the room was still shrouded in darkness. Her body trembled, every nerve tense as she listened for the noise that had startled her from her dark, dreamless sleep.

On the other side of the door, a scraping sound of metal against metal sent a shiver of raw terror through her. She willed her hand steady as she reached for her gun on the nightstand. When her fingers closed around the handle, a bone-deep chill shook her.

After sliding out of bed noiselessly, she tiptoed toward the door. The sound of a solid click told her the lock had been violated. She pressed herself against the wall as the door swung slowly open.

She heard him exhale softly, and her own breath froze in her lungs. A soft rustling sound, cloth against cloth, announced his entrance into the room. When he reached for the door to close it behind him, he nearly touched her arm and Kelsey felt her flesh crawl. She swallowed hard, trying to dislodge the fear that almost choked her.

As the shadowy figure moved deeper into the room toward the bed where moments ago Kelsey had slept unaware, her blood turned icy. Fresh terror gripped her when she saw he held some kind of club or weapon in his right hand. The horror of the moment immobilized her for precious seconds.

When she saw him bend over the bed, her survival instincts kicked in and an inner voice shouted, *Now!* With a burst of raw courage she never knew she possessed, Kelsey shouted, "Freeze!" At the same time she flicked the light switch on the wall beside her and leveled the gun at the intruder's broad back.

His arms were raised toward the ceiling, the bottle of wine swathed in a brown bag was suspended from his right hand. For a moment neither of them moved. When she'd yelled he'd thought his heart would stop and now it kicked back in with a heavy thud. When he slowly turned to her, the look on her face said she'd experienced a couple of cardiac tremors, as well.

"Ben!" she gasped.

"Good Lord," he sighed as he lowered his hands and tossed the bottle onto the bed. "You nearly gave me heart failure."

"You!" she shot back, quickly lowering the gun she seemed to notice for the first time was pointed at his chest. "You nearly scared me to death, Tanner! Haven't you ever heard of knocking?" she scolded. "My God, I could have shot you!" The breath whooshed out of her in a ragged gasp.

He watched the blood drain from her face, and for a second he feared she might faint. Moving to her side quickly, he took her hand and led her over to the bed, where she sat down woodenly.

"I did knock," he said. "Not very loudly, I'll admit, but I hadn't planned to startle you. After several minutes of waiting for you to hear me, I worried that you might be in some kind of trouble, so I took matters into my own hands."

"You know, now that I think about it, I think I did hear some kind of tapping noise," she said. "It must have been what finally wakened me."

"I could use a drink," he said. "How about you?"

She nodded numbly as he reached for the bottle of wine and withdrew it from the bag.

Kelsey was still sitting on the side of the bed when he returned from the bathroom with a half-filled glass of white wine.

"To your health," he said, handing her the glass and waiting for her to bring it to her lips before he pressed the bottle to his own mouth and tipped it up.

"And to yours," she countered, shoving the gun back into her purse. The blood came back to her face in a rush of color and her eyes began to shine. "Where have you been?" she demanded. But without giving him time to answer, she said, "What did you find out from McElroy? What about the loan shark? And the identity of Shannon's murderer—did Roger give you his name? And what the hell are you doing here?"

"Hey, hey, one question at a time," he chided gently. "It's been a long day, and in light of your reception, I'm beginning to think you didn't even miss me."

She clamped her lips in a way that didn't do a very good job of hiding her smile. "Pour," she ordered, and he filled the glass again and she drained it in two long swallows.

When she lowered her glass, Ben longed to kiss her shimmering lips, but the memory of the angry words that had passed between them the last time they'd been together stopped him from acting on the urge that felt as natural as breathing. He tipped the bottle up and took a long swallow.

Kelsey watched him, her eyes locked on his face, drinking in his rugged handsomeness, filling her senses with the sight of him. There was an endearing softness around his eyes, a tentative smile hovering at the corners of his mouth. At that moment she wanted nothing more than to see that smile in full bloom.

"I did miss you, Tanner," she murmured, her voice husky and rich with the emotion she saw shimmering in his eyes. "And you'll never know how glad I am that you're here. Even if you did scare ten years off my life." With her admission, she felt all the tension, all the strain of the past twenty-four hours, melt away and leave her body.

He reached for her and she went willingly into his embrace. "I missed you, too, Kelsey," he whispered, sending a thrill of desire through her. "And there's no place I'd rather be than here with you tonight."

She snuggled her face against his chest for a long moment. "But how did you know where I'd be?" she asked again, pulling reluctantly out of his arms. "Did you finally get my messages?"

"I didn't even know you'd called."

"I started leaving messages this morning," she admitted, her eyes captivated by his steady gaze. "I just couldn't let things stand the way we left them," she said softly. "I wanted to apologize. I left half a dozen messages for you at the precinct."

He touched her cheek. "After I left McElroy at the hospital, I didn't go back to my office."

"But why not?"

He pulled her closer. "Because this morning everything hit me, as well. I couldn't deal with the way we left things last night, either, and I came to the conclusion that the Chicago PD could probably function just fine without Ben Tanner for a day or two." He kissed her lightly.

"And I came to another conclusion," he said. "A much more important one. The simple fact is, I love you, Kelsey. You're the most important thing in my life. And if you'll give me another chance, I promise I'll never let anything come between us again."

Kelsey felt her heart swell with joy. Coherent speech seemed an impossibility. "Ben, I don't know... I don't know what to say..." she stammered.

"Just say you love me, too," he offered gently, the sensuous timbre of his voice sending desire through her. "Say you love me, Kelsey St. James, and that's all I'll ever need to know."

"I do love you, Ben," she said softly. Her simple admission seemed to release a longing in both of them, and they reached for each other hungrily. And in the pleasure of each other's arms, the horrors of the day and the uncertainties of the night disappeared.

THE SMELL OF fresh coffee roused her from a deep, satisfying sleep. Kelsey opened her eyes to discover that Ben was already up and dressed and that while she'd been sleeping, he'd evidently gone out and brought back a takeout breakfast for the two of them.

"Good morning, sunshine," Ben said playfully, planting a quick kiss on her forehead before easing down onto the bed beside her and pulling her back into his arms.

The feel of his lean muscled body pressed against hers brought back a rush of golden memories from last night, and her body ached again for his touch. Last night their lovemaking had gone from that first feverish frenzy of unbridled desire to a slow, gentle time of discovery and tenderness. Even now, Kelsey still felt the delightfully intoxicating effects of their mutual expressions of love.

"I trust you slept well," he said as he pushed the hair from her face.

"Never better, Detective," she purred, and nestled deeper into his arms. "And how about you?"

His response was a deliciously sexy smile. "Well, let's just say that if you're not up and out of that bed in ten minutes I might try to persuade you to stay there for the rest of the day."

She released a thready sigh, thinking that nothing could be more delightful than to spend endless hours wrapped in his arms. But when her gaze wandered to the wilted rose still laying on the dresser across the room, it served as a powerful reminder of the reality that awaited them just beyond the door.

Ben's eyes followed hers, and he sat up and handed her a cup of coffee. "You get dressed," he said solemnly. "I'll call the florist."

AN HOUR LATER, after they'd questioned the owner of Blossoms and Bows, Willowbend's only florist, most of Kelsey's suspicions had been confirmed. As she'd suspected, the rose had been ordered by phone and the caller had requested delivery. What Kelsey couldn't have predicted and wasn't prepared to hear was that the rose had been paid for with a credit card issued to Jennifer White.

Kelsey's hands were still shaking when she walked out of the florist and she and Ben got into her car to drive to Michael Grady's studio.

When Mike answered the door, Kelsey was stunned by how little he'd changed. He hadn't added a pound to his lean frame, and he still wore the heavy black-rimmed glasses he'd worn in high school.

He recognized Kelsey, as well, and seemed pleased to see her. When he ushered them into a small office, Kelsey remembered the room as one Miss Claire had designated as a dressing room. A large oak desk and a couple of wooden chairs had replaced the small wire baskets designed to hold the dancers' street clothes and shoes.

"Well, what brings you back to Willowbend, Kelsey?" Mike asked when they were all seated. "I must admit I was more than a little surprised to see you. I always thought you were one of the lucky ones."

Ben shot him a questioning glance.

"One of the ones who'd found a way out," Mike explained. "The natives say you have to fill your pockets with dirt when you leave or Willowbend will keep pulling you back."

"Well, I had my dreams," she said. Kelsey's pockets had been so filled with dreams that she hadn't had room for even a handful of Willowbend soil. And she'd seen most of those dreams come true, she told herself now. Perhaps it was time for some new dreams.

Glancing at Ben, she realized that her new dreams would have to be big enough for two.

"You look wonderful, Kelsey," Mike said. "City life agrees with you."

"And it looks like you're doing what you always wanted to do, Mike."

He nodded, smiling modestly. "Well, I've had to make a few compromises. I don't get a chance to do as many magazine spreads as I'd like, but I'm still working on it. Hey, wait a minute. Didn't I hear you'd become a cop or something?"

Kelsey smiled. "Or something," she muttered. "Mike, I want to ask you a few questions, would you mind?"

"Fire away, Officer," he quipped.

"When did you buy the studio?"

He didn't have to think. "August ninth of last year."

"Did you buy it from Claire Merriweather?"

Mike shook his head. "Oh, no. Why, Miss Claire's been gone . . . a year. Yes," he said, his voice fading a bit. "A year exactly tomorrow."

"Gone?" Ben asked.

"Passed away," Mike explained, his voice dropping a respectful notch.

The news that Claire Merriweather was dead stunned Kelsey. "But she wasn't old," Kelsey blurted out. "And dancing kept her in terrific shape."

Mike lowered his eyes and his voice. "Miss Claire didn't die of natural causes, Kelsey," he said softly.

"She was murdered?" Kelsey asked, her voice thin.

Mike shook his head sadly. "No, Miss Claire committed suicide. Right here in this house. Upstairs. Took an overdose of pills and died in her sleep. I guess that's why I got this place for a song. I didn't want it for a residence, and I guess with all the rumors no one else did, either.''

Kelsey found herself momentarily speechless.

"Do you know where we can reach Deirdre Merriweather?" Ben asked.

Mike looked at Kelsey, his eyes narrowed. "You haven't kept up with the local news at all, have you?"

Kelsey shook her head. "When Mom moved away, I guess I kind of lost touch. Besides I was never very close to Deirdre. After grammar school, I don't remember hearing much about her except something about her going to Europe to dance."

"Then you couldn't have known that I was engaged to Deirdre for a short while a few years ago," he said, his eyes reflecting a lasting pain. "Even when I was a young boy I always remember thinking she was the most beautiful girl I'd ever seen. All that blond hair, and that sweet face..." His wistful smile faded. "She bombed that audition in Europe. You know, my mother always maintained that ballet was more Miss Claire's dream than Deirdre's. Anyway, after she came back, Deirdre decided to change her name to Monique—she refused to even answer unless you called her by her new name."

"Go on, Mike," Kelsey urged.

"Well, Miss Claire kept Deirdre in private schools throughout high school, and after that she mortgaged everything she owned to send Deirdre to some exclusive dance academy in New York. Just after high school, I went to New York to enroll in an art school. Deirdre and I became reacquainted. I fell in love with her all over again, just as I had when we were in school.

But Deirdre—Monique—could never settle down. She was always so flighty, so flirty and wild. Do you remember?"

He didn't wait for her to answer but went on. "Anyway, we broke up eventually and I came back home. Within a year she was expelled from the dance academy, and she persuaded her mother to let her go to California to audition for a small role in a movie. From there, we all kind of lost track of her. There was some talk that she'd been in a couple of low-budget productions."

"Did she ever come home to visit her mother? Did you ever see or talk to her again, Mike?" Kelsey asked, leaning forward, eager for his answer.

He nodded. "She came back home for good about eighteen months ago. She was in a wheelchair. The doctors said she would be there for the rest of her life."

Kelsey gasped. "My God, Mike, what happened to her?"

"She'd had an accident. Lost the use of both her legs," he said, his voice low. "Permanently." He was silent for a moment, as though trying to regain his composure. Kelsey was glad his voice was stronger when he continued. "She would never talk about it, but according to what Miss Claire told my mother, it happened while she was living in Atlanta with a boyfriend she'd hooked up with in California."

"A car accident?" Ben asked.

Mike shook his head, his expression grim. "A fall. They say it was an accident . . ." he began doubtfully.

"But you don't believe it?" Kelsey put in.

"No," he said. "I don't. They say she fell from a fire escape one night while there was a wild party going on at her apartment."

Kelsey felt a chill shimmy up her spine. Ben glanced at her, but even the love she saw shining in his eyes couldn't dispel the chill that had settled deep inside her.

"Deirdre was a lot of things," Mike muttered, "but she was never clumsy."

"Where is Deirdre now?" Ben asked.

"She's gone," Mike answered, his voice a ragged whisper. "She took her own life the same night as her mother. They found them side by side in the sitting room upstairs."

No one said anything for several moments. Finally Kelsey rose and put her hand on Mike's shoulder. "I'm sorry," she said quietly.

He looked up at her gratefully. "When she came home I asked her again to marry me," he said softly. "But she refused, of course. Said she didn't need my pity. But it wouldn't have been pity, Kelsey," he insisted. "I still loved her and I wanted to marry her. I really did."

Kelsey's hand was still on his shoulder. "She was lucky to have had someone who loved her as much as you did, Mike."

"I still love her, Kelsey," he whispered. "I guess I always will."

At the door, Ben shook hands with Mike before he and Kelsey walked across the porch. Suddenly something occurred to Kelsey and she turned around. "Mike, did you know Deirdre's brother?"

Mike shook his head. "No one knew Cameron very well, I'm afraid. As a matter of fact, I'm surprised you remember him. Cameron was hospitalized for over twenty years."

Cameron, Kelsey thought, remembering his name and the incident in Miss Claire's backyard as if it had been yesterday.

"Why was he hospitalized?" Ben asked.

"He was diagnosed as a severe paranoid schizophrenic at an early age. After Deirdre's father died from a sudden heart attack, Miss Claire found herself all alone trying to deal with Cameron. She did pretty well most of the time. But finally, when Deirdre was only seven or eight, Cameron attacked her and Miss Claire decided she had to have him committed."

Kelsey did some quick mental math. "That would have been around the time of our recital," she said vaguely. "Mike, is Cameron still under treatment? Do you know what hospital he's in?"

He shook his head. "He's not in a hospital, Kelsey. Miss Claire brought him home about two years ago, but when Deirdre came home, he moved out. For a while, he held a job here in town at the school as a janitor or handyman, I think. But then I heard that he'd moved south. Gee, I really don't know what happened to him after that, Kelsey. Sorry I can't be more help."

"It's all right," she said. "And believe me, you have helped, you've helped a great deal."

BEFORE THEY LEFT the motel, Ben put in a call to the FBI. "They're running a check on Cameron Merriweather," he said as he hung up the phone. "We should have some answers by the time we get back to

Chicago. If Deirdre's brother is in a state hospital, we may be able to get an interview with him.''

Ben's next call was to his office. Kelsey packed her bag and changed into cotton shorts and a cool blouse while Ben left a message for Gil. She couldn't help but feel defeated. Her trip to Willowbend had been fraught with sadness and disappointment. Claire and Deirdre Merriweather, the only two people who could have possibly shed light on the connection between herself and the murdered women, were both dead.

"Looks like we'll get an indictment on McElroy by the end of the week," Ben said as he hung up the phone. "His attorney, Ms. Overholt, has convinced him to cop a plea. He's admitted to breaking into your office by making a copy of Shannon's key. He's admitted he was paid to start the fire in your building and he's named the loan shark. Your prescription was found in his apartment. Did you know he was hooked on prescription drugs?''

Kelsey shook her head.

"He admitted his addiction to the doctors. It sounds like Roger is talking loud and long to save his skin.''

Kelsey's eyes widened with anticipation. "But what about Shannon's murderer? Did Roger identify him, as well?''

Ben shook his head. "I'm afraid not, honey.''

Kelsey swallowed her disappointment. "Damn it,'' she said. "Then why did he say he could?''

"The loan shark and McElroy must have thought you needed an extra inducement to force you to cooperate with them. They only wanted their money, Kelsey. People like that will say and do anything to get what they want.''

"Well," Kelsey sighed, reaching for her bag. "I guess we'd better get going."

He reached for her bag. "Hey, don't you even want to know the good news?"

Kelsey blinked. Her final rose had been delivered, three women had been murdered and she and Ben and the FBI seemed no closer today than they'd been yesterday to discovering the identity of the man who still stalked her—in all of that, how could there be any good news? Kelsey wondered.

"The good news," Ben said, as though reading her mind, "is that Douglas Hughes will soon be on his way to jail."

Kelsey's startled expression asked the question.

"He's our loan shark, Kelsey," Ben explained. "And with the charges of extortion, money laundering and assault hanging over his head, he should be gone a good long time."

"Has he been arrested?"

"A warrant has been issued, but I don't think they've picked him up yet."

Her mind began to whirl.

"There's nothing to indicate that he's our murderer," Ben added. "His alibi held up. And he has no connection that we know of with the other victims."

Kelsey nodded uncertainly. "None that we know of," she affirmed. "I just know I'll feel a whole lot safer once he's firmly behind bars."

Ben tossed her bag into the back seat and held the car door open while she climbed in. "If he hasn't been picked up by the time we get back to Chicago," he said, "I promise you I'll go after him myself."

KELSEY COULD HEAR the phone ringing as she fumbled with the keys to unlock her front door. "Hello," she said breathlessly into the receiver. "Yes, hold on. I think he's right behind me." Ben walked through the door as she spoke.

"That's very interesting," Kelsey heard Ben saying. "A private home. Okay, give me the name and number."

Kelsey slid a pen and paper toward him.

"Glenaire," Ben wrote, underlining the name twice before jotting down the number. "Thanks," he said and hung up.

"Was that Gil?" she asked.

"No, it was the duty officer relaying a message from the FBI. Mike Grady was right. Cameron Merriweather was released into his mother's custody just a little less than two years ago. But after his mother and sister died, he seemed to have disappeared."

Kelsey bent numbly into a chair beside the phone, her disappointment shoving her down like a leaden hand.

Ben picked up the phone again, dialed information and in a moment Kelsey heard him talking to someone at Glenaire Hospital, where he demanded to speak to an administrator.

Miss Marple leaped up onto Kelsey's lap and Sherlock rested his head on her knee. She petted them both idly as she listened to Ben trying to garner information about Cameron Merriweather.

In a moment he hung up the phone. His jaw was set when he said, "Well, it looks like I've got to go see a man about a court order."

"I take it you weren't able to find out anything about Cameron through the administrator?"

Ben shook his head. "Private hospitals pride themselves on discretion."

"If we only had a current address, a phone number..."

"And a photograph," he added.

"Why a photograph?"

"If we had a recent photo, maybe we could jog some memories."

Kelsey caught his meaning. "Like maybe the memories of the clerks at Jan's House of Flowers?"

"Exactly."

"But do you think you can you get a court order at this time of night?" she asked. "It's nearly five."

"It may take some doing," Ben said. "Let's go." He reached for her hand.

"Go ahead," Kelsey said. "I'm exhausted. I want to take a long shower and unpack. You go get your court order, and by the time you get back, I just might feel human again."

He smiled and brushed an errant strand of blond hair from her cheek. "When I get back, I'll take you to dinner. We've never really had a proper date, you know."

She returned his smile. "That sounds wonderful. Ben, do you really think Cameron Merriweather could be the killer?"

He put his arm around her shoulder as they walked together to the door. "Right now I'd say he makes as good a suspect as anyone. He was connected to each victim, albeit in a roundabout way. Regardless, he's a fresh lead."

"And if he was released two years ago," Kelsey put in, "the hospital must have thought he was functioning well enough to be on his own. If we could find him, maybe he could tell us something that could give us some other leads."

"Always the optimist," he teased.

"Always the investigator," she corrected, before kissing him lightly and opening the door.

"Lock this," he ordered, "and don't go out of this house. Watch out for her, Sherlock."

"We'll be fine, Detective." Kelsey smiled, his concern warming her. "Go see your judge and get that court order."

She stood at the door and watched him drive away, realizing guiltily that, if not for Shannon's death, she might never have met the man who had so completely captured her heart.

"But you understand, don't you, my friend?" she whispered. At that moment, Kelsey felt something rub against her leg. Tears stung her eyes as she bent down to stroke the small, furry fluffball that was looking up at her lovingly. "Oh, Dolly," she cried, gathering the white kitten into her arms. "I'm so glad I have you."

AFTER HER SHOWER Kelsey gave in to her physical exhaustion and lay down on the bed and closed her eyes. She'd meant to rest for only ten minutes or so, but at the sound of the doorbell and Sherlock's furious barking, she glanced at the illuminated numbers on the clock beside the bed and saw that it was nearly seven.

As she hurried down the hallway, Sherlock continued to bark and the cats skittered into hiding. Kelsey glanced through the small half-moon window in the front door but didn't see anyone. She opened the door and scanned the sidewalk up and down the block, but other than the neighbor across the street mowing his lawn, she didn't see a soul.

A sound in the direction of the kitchen drew Kelsey's attention to the back door and she hurried toward it. She could see through the window that Gil Montoya was standing outside, tapping lightly on the door.

"Gil," she said breathlessly as she swung the door open wide. "Did you ring the front doorbell."

Gil nodded as he slid his sunglasses up onto the top of his head. "I saw your car, but when no one answered I decided to come around back."

"You caught me napping," Kelsey explained as she ushered him inside.

When she closed the door behind him, Gil seemed suddenly uneasy. He shifted nervously from one foot to the other, speaking rapidly as he explained, "Ben asked me to swing by on my way home and let you know that he's still trying to track down a judge for the court order to force Glenaire to fax a copy of Cameron's release papers, current address and a photograph."

Kelsey hoped Ben could obtain the court order in time.

"Well, I guess I better get going," Gil said as he backed toward the door. "Don't worry, Kelsey," he added. "The entire homicide department, the FBI and half the plainclothes cops in the city are looking for this guy. He's bound to make a mistake. No one is perfect, you know. We'll catch him sooner or later. It's time he took his fall."

After Gil left, Kelsey replayed everything he'd said. With the tremendous effort being exerted by the authorities, why did she still feel so vulnerable? She tried to make herself feel better by remembering what Gil had said about every criminal making a mistake eventually. "It's time he took his fall," Gil had said. But would it be too late? Kelsey wondered. Would his first mistake be her last?

Kelsey decided she needed to get busy, to keep her mind and her body occupied while she waited for Ben. She'd surprise him and cook him dinner, she decided. She'd set the dining room table, even use the good silver. She was reaching for the silverware box in the buffet drawer in the hallway when she noticed a piece of paper halfway under the front door.

It looked as though someone had tried to shove a note under the door but hadn't completely succeeded. When Kelsey bent to pick it up, she found that she had to tug to pull the plain white envelope through the small slit under the door. At last she succeeded.

When had the note been delivered, she wondered. Surely it hadn't been there when she and Ben had come home from Willowbend. And she hadn't noticed it a few moments earlier when she'd thought someone was at the front door, either.

Why hadn't Sherlock barked if someone had slipped it under the door while she was sleeping? A chill of alarm slithered through her as another possibility presented itself: perhaps the envelope had been delivered while she was at the back door talking to Gil. Perhaps Gil himself had delivered it. Kelsey dismissed that last thought as desperate paranoia as she ripped the envelope open.

Her hand trembled as she reached in to withdraw the contents. "Dear God," she whispered, her heart pounding. *Ballet tickets!* Through eyes blurred with fear she read the small print and realized the tickets were for a performance of the Chicago Ballet Company at Auditorium Theater downtown. The date on the tickets was today's date. And the time of the performance was eight o'clock.

Chapter Fourteen

The officer on duty in homicide was cooperative and polite, but he couldn't give Kelsey the name of the judge who'd finally agreed to give Ben the court order.

"Please," Kelsey begged him. "It's vital that I reach Detective Tanner as soon as possible."

"Look, Ms. St. James, I'd give you the name if I had it, but I don't. Ben's in his own car and he hasn't got a radio. The best we can do is wait for him to call or come in. When he does, I'll personally see to it that he gets your message."

"All right," Kelsey relented. "Tell him I'm going to the ballet. Auditorium Theater, eight o'clock."

"The ballet?" the officer asked.

"Yes," Kelsey said, her voice tremulous. "He'll know what I mean. Tell him to meet me in the balcony, east side, private box."

"Ms. St. James, are you in some kind of trouble?"

The temptation was great to tell the officer everything, but Kelsey feared the show of force that she knew could be mustered in a situation like this. Shannon's killer was clever, meticulous. As Gil had reminded her, so far the murderer had managed to outsmart the FBI and the police in three different states. If he so much as sniffed a setup, he'd disappear. Although his disappearance might mean that her own life had been spared, no one would ever be able to predict when or where he might strike again.

Kelsey could never live with knowing she'd been even inadvertently responsible for another young woman's death.

"No. But thank you, Officer. I'm fine," Kelsey lied. "Just be sure he gets the message. It's extremely important." Her hand trembled as she replaced the receiver.

FORTY MINUTES LATER Kelsey was in her car, headed downtown. The traffic going into the city wasn't bad for a Friday night. She glanced in the rearview mirror at her reflection. The makeup she'd hurriedly applied couldn't conceal the inner turmoil that robbed her checks of all natural color. The chignon at her nape looked surprisingly sleek, considering the shaky hands that had arranged it.

Unconsciously she smoothed the skirt of the black spaghetti-strap gown she wore. She'd chosen black for only one reason: her gun fit perfectly into her black beaded bag.

It was just as well that the house lights had already been dimmed by the time Kelsey arrived at the auditorium. The tuxedoed usher spoke in muted whispers and used subtle gestures as he led her to the upper balcony seat that matched the number on her ticket.

As they walked, Kelsey made a mental note of every lighted exit, knowing that familiarity with each possible escape route could be vital.

As she slipped into the private box, she reached for the usher's sleeve as he was leaving. "My name is Kelsey St. James," she informed him. "A gentleman may be looking for me later. Please be sure he knows where I'm seated."

The apprehension that washed over her when the usher disappeared and she found herself all alone in the private box was nearly nauseating. Kelsey forced a deep, shaky breath and sat down, every nerve tingling as she waited for her eyes to adjust to the semidarkness.

Chancing a glimpse at the stage, Kelsey estimated the private box was at least two hundred feet above the dancers. A familiar knot of anxiety began to form in the pit of her stomach. The dancers moved across the stage in a swirl of graceful color, but Kelsey could only sneak an occasional peek at the production that captivated the rest of the audience.

On any other night, Kelsey could have at least appreciated the music that emanated from the orchestra pit, but tonight the notes that rose and fell as the music moved relentlessly toward the end of the score served only as a morbid reminder of the passage of time.

To Kelsey, time was both an enemy and a friend. With each moment that passed, the killer's plan moved closer to completion. But the longer he waited to keep this deadly rendezvous, the greater the chances that Ben would arrive, Kelsey told herself.

She started when the house lights rose at intermission. The strain of waiting, of watching, had turned her palms clammy. Her neck and shoulders burned with the accumulated tension. Her head hurt and her stomach churned. The movement and noise of the crowd milling below and around her outside the box was maddening. Her eyes flitted from one man to the next, and all the while she wondered when and how the killer would reveal himself.

She sat rigidly, clutching her purse on her lap. Just when she'd decided to make her way down to the lobby to find a phone and contact Ben again, the house lights dimmed. Kelsey cursed the indecision that had caused her to hesitate. Not knowing if the killer was waiting, she decided she dared not risk moving through the darkened theater.

The music rose again and Kelsey glanced down at the stage. The ballet, *Romeo and Juliet,* had always been one of her favorites, and for a brief moment as she watched the nimble dancers moving across the stage, acting out the drama of the star-crossed lovers, she could almost forget why she was here.

A sudden movement at the back of the box startled her. An usher emerged from behind the curtains and handed her a note. With a flick of a tiny penlight, he illuminated the words. "Sit tight," the note read. "I'm on my way. Ben."

A flicker of concern passed over the usher's face when Kelsey released a ragged breath. "Are you all right, miss?" he whispered.

"Yes, yes," she managed. "Just fine. Please show Detective Tanner to this box the moment he arrives."

The usher nodded and disappeared without a sound. Kelsey closed her eyes. Her arms and legs felt weak. She inhaled deeply, willing the strength back into her quivering muscles.

When she opened her eyes, she gasped at the man she saw standing over her. But his hand, clutching a sticky, adhesive substance, closed over her mouth before she could cry out.

"Hush, Kelsey," he ordered, his voice slippery as silk. The bitter taste and smell of adhesive choked her as the moleskin was pressed firmly across her lips. He grabbed her arms, pinning them behind her with such force that she thought they'd be snapped from their sockets. She struggled against him as he lifted her from her seat and shoved her against the gilded railing that surrounded the private box.

The music reached a crescendo, drowning out her muffled shrieks. Her breath came in ragged gasps through her nose. Her eyes felt as though they would bulge out of her head as he bent her over the railing. Fear flooded her as dizzying panic swept her dangerously close to unconsciousness. To her horror, to her disgust and outrage, she realized she was about to faint.

Her worst nightmare could not compare to the terror that flooded her as she stared down at the stage below. She was going to die, her mind screamed. Cameron Merriweather was going to win and she would be helpless to stop him. "All fall down," he whispered as he pressed her harder.

The blackness swirled closer, tugging at her senses, and for one breathless moment Kelsey considered giving in to it, welcoming its soft, black oblivion.

"Breathe, Kelsey," she ordered herself. *"Breathe!"*

"All fall down. All fall down. The last little domino is about to fall down." The taunting whisper filled Kelsey's mind, drowning out her own thoughts. The dizziness swept through her again and she closed her eyes.

Suddenly, a barked command coming from somewhere deep inside her mind grabbed her senses and ripped them from Cameron's possession. *"Look down, Kelsey,"* the voice commanded. *"Look down. Face your fears and live!"* It was the sound of the voice she'd spent a lifetime resenting, but tonight it was the voice of survival. Her father's voice was ordering her to fight back, and Kelsey obeyed.

She opened her eyes and began to fight again in earnest against her tormentor, kicking and twisting and bucking with all her might.

The commotion above them caused a few startled members of the audience below the box to finally notice the drama being played out above them. At the same moment the musical score ebbed, a woman's shrill scream split the air. The music died with a discordant screech. The house lights went up.

At that moment, with strength born of sheer determination, Kelsey twisted free of Cameron's grip and swung her body around to face him.

Momentarily stunned by her strength, he stumbled backward. She lunged for her purse and grabbed her gun. But Cameron snatched it before she could take aim and tossed it over the railing. A shot rang out as the gun discharged and the sounds of the audience seized by uncertainty and panic exploded like a clap of sudden thunder.

With his attention momentarily distracted by the melee below, Kelsey ripped the moleskin from her mouth. The air rushed into her lungs at the same moment she emitted a slashing scream.

"Damn you!" Cameron hissed as he lunged for her, but Kelsey was too quick and blocked his attack with a sharp kick to his groin. As he collapsed in pain, Kelsey raced out of the box. To her horror, she saw that the jam of terrified people trying to escape had sealed off the exits that led down to the lobby.

She heard Cameron getting to his feet and she turned and raced toward the stairwell, kicking off her high-heeled shoes as she ran. She hit the door running and shoved it open, only to see the stairway leading down clogged with more people. She had two choices: fight the crowd and possibly endanger the lives of countless others, or go up.

She made her choice without a second thought. Perhaps Cameron would be too confused, too panicked himself, to come after her. As she raced up the first flight of concrete stairs, her hopes ran high. But just as quickly they were dashed when, at the next flight, she chanced a peek below and saw Cameron charging the steps two at a time after her.

Another flight and another. She could hear his footsteps rushing madly behind her, his maniacal curses ricocheting wildly around the concrete that enclosed them. Another story and finally a door, a metal door painted red and bearing the stenciled warning Keep Out.

Kelsey hit the crash bar with all her might. The startling scream of an alarm sliced the heavy summer air.

She slammed the door behind her, but knew that she had no way of locking him out.

Desperately scanning the rooftop, Kelsey was struck by how starkly alone she was. Shaking off the defeating thought, she ran for a cluster of aluminum ducts about three feet high and hid behind them. Her shelter would only be temporary, she told herself when she heard the door to the rooftop crash open.

"Where are you, Kelsey?" Cameron shrieked. "You can't hide forever. It's no use. The dance is over. All fall down!" he cried. "All fall down!"

A shudder of fear and revulsion shook her as his demented words hung heavily on the warm night air.

She peeked around the metal stack that she was crouched behind to see him moving toward her. Another six feet and he would be upon her.

Desperately her mind formulated a plan. If she could somehow divert his attention, lure him past her, she could try to outrun him to the door. She was buying time, precious time, for the crowds on the stairs to disperse, for help to arrive.

Cautiously and without a sound, she edged backward, slipping around the corner of the stack, being careful not to reveal her hiding place. When she was sure he would not see the motion, she plucked off her earrings and flung them as far as she could away from her.

The explosion of a gunshot accompanied the sound of the earrings skittering across the rooftop. Despite herself, Kelsey cried out. *Dear God, he has a gun!* her startled mind shrieked.

She might be able to outrun Cameron, she told herself. But once she left her hiding place, she'd be an open target.

Another glance around the stack told her she had no choice. The diversion had only distracted Cameron for a moment, and now he was moving toward her again. Taking a quick breath for courage, Kelsey dashed from her hiding place and ran hell-bent for the door. She felt the bullet whiz past her ear before she heard the startling retort. Stumbling toward the door, she reached for the metal handle to keep from falling. Another shot rang out, and Kelsey felt the vibration when the bullet nicked the door.

"Stop!" he commanded. "Turn around, Kelsey."

She felt his presence right behind her. She knew he had his gun trained squarely on her back. She held her breath and turned around. The victorious smile she saw tilting his thin lips sent a shiver of sheer terror down her spine.

"See? What did I tell you, Deirdre?" he whispered. "I told you I would win."

Kelsey trembled; his madness terrified her.

"This way," he ordered with a quick movement of the gun.

Kelsey moved cautiously away from the door. He edged up beside her and jabbed the gun into her ribs. "This is better," he rasped. "So much better. So much higher than the balcony. Keep moving," he commanded, jabbing her again, sending a sharp pain shooting through her side.

Like a deserted country road in the moonlight, the edge of the roof was defined in liquid darkness. Tremors of fear shook every nerve in Kelsey's body as Cameron shoved her closer and closer toward the edge, toward certain death.

"Why?" she gasped. "Why are you doing this, Cameron?"

"Shut up," he growled. "Shut up, Deirdre!" he shrieked. "You can't stop me. I win. I win. You have to go away now. All the dancers are gone. No more performances. Mother is free. She's mine now."

"It won't bring them back," Kelsey cried. "Listen to me! Your mother and Deirdre...they're dead, Cameron. Even after you kill me, they'll still be gone."

They were only a matter of a few dozen feet from the edge of the building when he grabbed her arm and shoved her. Her heart nearly stopped when she stumbled.

"They aren't gone, Kelsey," he insisted, but his voice rang with his confusion, and Kelsey clung to it, her only thread of hope.

"Yes they are, Cameron. Didn't anyone tell you? Didn't you know?"

"But Mother can't be gone," Cameron insisted. "She's waiting for me at the house in Willowbend. Now get up," he ordered her as he grabbed her again and hauled her to her feet. "Move!" he shouted. "It's your turn. All fall down, all fall down," he chanted.

Kelsey moved slowly toward the edge, but when she was no more than a few feet from disaster she stopped and whirled around to face him.

"Your mother is dead," she said evenly. "Deirdre is dead. It's all over, Cameron. All over."

"Mother isn't gone!" he screamed. His eyes were glistening, and a sheen of sweat had risen on his cheeks and forehead. "Deirdre had only taken her away. But it's all over now. And I win. Now Deirdre has to give her back. When all the dancers have gone, when they've all fallen down and the stage lights go out, it will be just Mother and me again, together. The way we used to be before Deirdre came along and spoiled things.''

Kelsey watched the madness consume him. ''All fall down. All fall down. You have to die, Kelsey. Move!''

Kelsey stood her ground. Something Ben had told her about the ritual, the sequence that ruled the serial killer's actions, came back to her in a flash of insight.

''Then shoot,'' she challenged him. ''Go ahead, Cameron, kill me now. I won't walk to the edge, and if you try to force me, I'll take you down with me and then you'll never see your mother again.''

His eyes blazed. ''I'll kill you,'' he snarled through clenched teeth. ''Don't try to bluff me, Kelsey,'' he said as he pulled back the hammer and took aim. ''I heard all those theories the same as you did. But they're wrong. The FBI, Ben Tanner, all of them. The only thing that matters is that you all die and I'll kill you one way or the other.''

When the door to the rooftop burst open, Kelsey shouted, ''Ben! Look out! He's got a gun!'' She dived for the ground as Cameron squeezed the trigger. When she looked up, he was lunging at her. At that moment, she rolled to avoid his attack and he went staggering toward the roof's edge.

And as Cameron stumbled and fell over the edge of the building, his tormented screams shattered the night air, echoing for what seemed to be a lifetime before they were abruptly stilled.

In the space of a heartbeat, Ben was beside her. Kelsey flew into his arms, shaking uncontrollably, her quiet sobs tearing at his heart.

"You're safe," he assured her. "It's over. I'm here, Kelsey. It's all over."

THE FOLLOWING MONDAY, Mike Grady was the only mourner in attendance when the body of Cameron Merriweather, aka Gilbert Montoya, was laid to rest beside his mother and his sister in the small cemetery above the river that ran through the town of Willowbend.

After the services, Mike called Kelsey St. James to report that he'd found evidence that someone had broken into the upstairs rooms of the studio and spent the night there.

"Do you think it was Gil?" Kelsey asked when Ben hung up the phone and they walked together through her kitchen and out onto the patio.

"You mean Cameron?"

Kelsey nodded as she sank down into the lawn chair. "Without a doubt."

She slid her finger around the edge of the tumbler filled with iced tea and stared into the dark, amber liquid. "No wonder the killer seemed to always be one step ahead of the police," she said, suppressing the shudder. "Gil was there. All the time. He knew our every move, our every lead."

"And the irony is that the real Gil Montoya would probably have made a very fine police officer," Ben said.

Kelsey stared down at the FBI report on Gil Montoya, a young man whose only mistake had been his decision to change careers. A man who, on finding himself alone after his wife and only daughter were killed in an automobile accident, had decided to enroll in the Atlanta police academy.

The records showed that for two years Gil had been an exemplary cadet who made few mistakes. One look at his records and the Chicago Police Department was only too glad to accept him into their program.

But what the records couldn't show was the friendship Gil had entered into while still at the academy, the fateful friendship with the drifter he'd hired to do odd jobs around his home. A young man about his same age, same height, same weight and skin tone. Cameron Merriweather.

The neighbors would have taken note had the nice young cop at the end of the street suddenly disappeared, but when the handyman stopped coming around, no one seemed to notice.

Little did they know that a killer without a conscience had stolen Gilbert Montoya's life and his identity, that he would stalk and murder three innocent young women in an effort to defeat his sister and bring his dead mother back to life.

Epilogue

Kelsey pulled her Chevy up into the loading zone and shut off the engine. For a moment she could only stare in amazement at the place where only a short three months ago there had been nothing more than a heap of charred rubble.

Though she was still only a tenant, seeing the brand-new Printer's Row building filled her with pride. Her office had been painted on Tuesday, Nelson had issued her new insurance policy on Wednesday and today she was ready to move in.

A sharp horn blast from the moving truck that had pulled up behind her made Kelsey jump and scattered her thoughts in a million directions. Glancing into her side mirror, she saw the driver jump out of the cab of the truck. He was a big man and he was headed straight for her.

Without hesitation, she climbed out of her car and slammed the door, braced for his challenge.

"Hey, lady, can't you read? You're parked in a loading zone."

With a hand planted firmly on each hip, Kelsey stared at him without blinking. "And just what are you going to do about it, buddy? Call a cop?" she shot back.

"Hmm. Good idea," the driver said, his smoky gray eyes narrowing. "You wouldn't happen to know where I could find one, would you?"

She crooked her little finger and motioned him closer. "Well, I used to know a cop," she said, "a really good one. But he retired. Went into business with his wife. Tanner and Tanner, a couple of PIs. Ever hear of them?"

"The name does sound vaguely familiar."

She smiled. "Don't know if they could help you out, but I could ask them."

"You think you could?" he asked.

"Oh, sure," she purred seductively, sidling up to him and running one slender fingertip slowly down his cheek. "Mr. Tanner's a close friend of mine. I know I can work something out with him."

Ben caught her finger in his fist gently and brought it slowly to his lips and kissed it. "Do you promise?" he murmured, his gaze locked lovingly on her face.

"You know I do," she whispered, sliding her hands around his neck and closing her lips over his, savoring the sweet, sensual kiss of her partner, her husband and her friend.

HARLEQUIN®

I N T R I G U E®

Ski through glitzy Aspen with the King of Rock 'n' Roll
for the hottest—yet most mysteriously chilling—
August of 1994 ever!

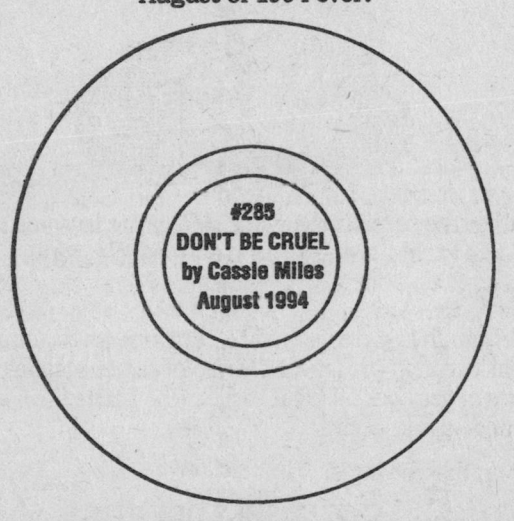

**#285
DON'T BE CRUEL
by Cassie Miles
August 1994**

Gina Robinson headed for glittering Aspen to purchase
her uncle's Elvis memorabilia…only to find herself
snowbound with Conner "Hound Dog" Hobarth. The two
built a cozy cabin fire destined to lead somewhere very
special. Unfortunately, the morning after, they found
Gina's uncle dead on the premises and discovered the law
thought the lovebirds had spent the night committing
murder!

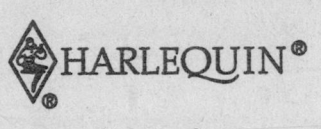

WEDDING SONG
Vicki Lewis Thompson

Kerry Muldoon has encountered more than her share of happy brides and grooms. She and her band—the Honeymooners—play at all the wedding receptions held in romantic Eternity, Massachusetts!

Kerry longs to walk down the aisle one day—with sexy recording executive Judd Roarke. But Kerry's dreams of singing stardom threaten to tear apart the fragile fabric of their union....

WEDDING SONG, available in August from Temptation, is the third book in Harlequin's new cross-line series, **WEDDINGS, INC.** Be sure to look for the fourth book, **THE WEDDING GAMBLE,** by Muriel Jensen (Harlequin American Romance #549), coming in September.

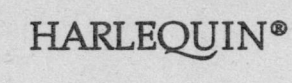 **HARLEQUIN®**

Don't miss these Harlequin favorites by some of our most distinguished authors!
And now you can receive a discount by ordering two or more titles!

HT #25525	THE PERFECT HUSBAND by Kristine Rolofson	$2.99 ☐
HT #25554	LOVERS' SECRETS by Glenda Sanders	$2.99 ☐
HP #11577	THE STONE PRINCESS by Robyn Donald	$2.99 ☐
HP #11554	SECRET ADMIRER by Susan Napier	$2.99 ☐
HR #03277	THE LADY AND THE TOMCAT by Bethany Campbell	$2.99 ☐
HR #03283	FOREIGN AFFAIR by Eva Rutland	$2.99 ☐
HS #70529	KEEPING CHRISTMAS by Marisa Carroll	$3.39 ☐
HS #70578	THE LAST BUCCANEER by Lynn Erickson	$3.50 ☐
HI #22256	THRICE FAMILIAR by Caroline Burnes	$2.99 ☐
HI #22238	PRESUMED GUILTY by Tess Gerritsen	$2.99 ☐
HAR #16496	OH, YOU BEAUTIFUL DOLL by Judith Arnold	$3.50 ☐
HAR #16510	WED AGAIN by Elda Minger	$3.50 ☐
HH #28719	RACHEL by Lynda Trent	$3.99 ☐
HH #28795	PIECES OF SKY by Marianne Willman	$3.99 ☐

Harlequin Promotional Titles

#97122	LINGERING SHADOWS by Penny Jordan	$5.99 ☐
	(limited quantities available on certain titles)	

	AMOUNT	$
DEDUCT:	10% DISCOUNT FOR 2+ BOOKS	$
	POSTAGE & HANDLING	$
	($1.00 for one book, 50¢ for each additional)	
	APPLICABLE TAXES*	$_____
	TOTAL PAYABLE	$_____
	(check or money order—please do not send cash)	

To order, complete this form and send it, along with a check or money order for the total above, payable to Harlequin Books, to: **In the U.S.:** 3010 Walden Avenue, P.O. Box 9047, Buffalo, NY 14269-9047; **In Canada:** P.O. Box 613, Fort Erie, Ontario, L2A 5X3.

Name: _____

Address:_____City: _____

State/Prov.: _____ Zip/Postal Code: _____

*New York residents remit applicable sales taxes.
 Canadian residents remit applicable GST and provincial taxes..

HBACK-JS